NO LONGER DRIFTING

by

Loretta Jackson *Vickie Britton*

Loretta Jackson & Vickie Britton

1-14-06

WHISKEY CREEK PRESS

www.whiskeycreekpress.com

Published by
WHISKEY CREEK PRESS

P.O. Box 51052
Casper, WY   82605-1052
307-334-3165
www.whiskeycreekpress.com

ISBN **1-59374-020-4**

Printed in the United States of America

NO LONGER DRIFTING

An Anthology by

Loretta Jackson and Vickie Britton

Credits: *The Sea God* took first place in the Mocha Memoirs Summer Writing Contest 2002; *Bound or Free* first appeared in The Family, 1989, Honorable Mention, Catholic Press Award, 1990; *Do You Take...?* First published by Kansas Quarterly, 1990, winner of the Second Seaton Award; *The Peacock on the Shelf*, first appeared in Writer's Journal, 1993; *The Big Exception*, Compassion Magazine, 1988; *An Act of Mercy*, Compassion Magazine, 1988; *The New Year*, The Family, 1991,*Trolls*, first place, Ebooks on the net Electryfying Mystery Contest, 2002.

Dedication

To Anita Sitting Up, with love.

INTRODUCTION

Grief, a tragic flaw, failure to see the truth, immobilizes the characters in these stories that Vickie Britton and Loretta Jackson tell with such heart and vividness. Each presents an obstacle that makes progress impossible.

The challenge can be caused by loss, like in *The Sea God* or it can be simply a failure to change and grow, like in *Adrift*. Whatever the problem, no easy answer exists and it looms threatening and impassable. Each character is forced to take some action or face the results of avoidance: unhappiness, loss of inner peace, or even of life itself.

I immediately became a party to every struggle, many that every person sooner or later must face. I found myself cheering the lead character on and learning something in the process.

Audrey Sallman

Sunlight Glints upon the placid water.
The stalwart boatman glides and dreams, content,
Until the storm that stirs him from his slumber
Breaks, and tossed by waves he takes command.
He places hand to helm, no longer drifting.

Table of Contents

No Longer Drifting
Jackson-Britton

When it seemed Nellie had but one option, she discovered in her "failure" how really to be free.

BOUND OR FREE

Voices surrounded Nellie threatening her like spurts of wind bent on total destruction. Her son's voice, trained by tedious practice to assume a tone of calm authority, and her daughter's voice, even more certain, never allowing for margins of error. Why did they speak in front of her as if she could no longer think or feel?

Snatches from Jane: "Mother's not capable of…can't live alone now."

Snatches from John. She knew his gray eyes would be as somber as if he were calling in a note at the bank.

No Longer Drifting
Jackson-Britton

"We can't...Mother should..."

Nellie's dark eyes remained locked on her shoes, drab, old shoes with bulging tops and the heavy-tread soles Jane insisted upon. Old woman's shoes!

Once Nellie had looked down at white sandals, often carelessly abandoned on rug and beach; or spike heels that danced lithely half the night. Nellie's feet now seemed immobile in their bulky, black encasements. Where had the time gone? Was it really Nellie Darby sitting here...listening?

Alone after Marvin had died, Nellie had selected the very best universities for her three children, the very best jobs. Only Linden, her oldest son, had evaded her careful molding. The other two were children to be proud of—the very images of prosperity and attainment. The logic she had always held up for them to follow now frightened her. The voices said, "It's best for Mother...Villa Rest Home is tops...She'll get the very best of care."

Nellie's own reasoning told her she had no options. John had an enormous home and no children, but she could not live with him and his wife amid the high-toned guests that swarmed year round. These personages were as much a part of their lives as the antique chandeliers and the crystal glass.

And Jane tried to juggle family and job—a success at both, but so busy, so very busy that she had no time cut out of it for Nellie.

Nellie straightened up. She would do what must be done. Make it easy for them. Pretend to be in good spirits. After all, she had fallen down, hadn't she? The fact was she could not live alone any longer.

The phone rang.

"Mother." Jane balanced the receiver between ear and shoulder. "It's Linden."

Nellie suddenly wanted to talk to Linden, but Jane turned away, grasping the receiver tightly. After a long silence, she said, "There's no need for you to come back. John and I will take care of Mother. There's absolutely nothing for you to do."

"Let me talk to him," John said. Sister and brother stood close, John, burly next to small, slender Jane.

More voices. Nellie's eyes dropped to her shoes again, then roamed over Marvin's gun case and to the brass stands that housed her flowers. She remembered when Jane had to get a chair to water the Swedish Ivy.

Jane said, "Linden will just cause trouble. He'll make a fool of all of us the way he did when Father died."

John nodded. "But what can we do? He's almost here."

"What does he want to come back for?"

"I don't know." John paused. "To top it all off, he's driving that monster of a truck. He probably won't make it past Austin."

* * *

Moving to the Home, Nellie thought, was a little bit like dying. She watched quietly as Jane sorted the contents of the big China cabinet. "You won't need all of this. I'll just box most of it for charity."

As Jane tossed books, mementoes, and pictures into a box to be discarded, Nellie longed to stop her. But Jane was right—most of it was unnecessary, just clutter.

Jane began packing Nellie's books, books collected with love and care over a lifetime. Dramas, mysteries, classics. "Doesn't anyone want to read them?"

Jane, absorbed in her chores hadn't even heard the question. "I guess I can find a place for these somewhere," she said, rising, and taking the three, large photographs of the children, which had for years hung over the fireplace. Jane's hall closet, Nellie supposed, never again would they hold a place of honor.

Nellie stared at the blank space upon the wall where they had hung, and she could see them as well as if they were still there. Jane and John in graduation gowns—clean-cut, bright, smiling. How proud they had always made her! She had spent hours bragging about the two of them to her friends, but not so with Linden. Linden had never graduated, not even from high school, but she had taken his picture just the same, Lind in blue jeans and beard, standing by the sea.

Linden loved the ocean. "It's freedom," he said, "from all of this!" Nellie could close her eyes and visualize his little beach house, the boat, the shop filled with shells, sponges and sea treasures. He supported himself with the shop, and on week ends he played his guitar at the little beachside cafe, which was always crammed with hopeful musicians. Sometimes Linden reminded her of Marvin, of their early years of marriage. The younger children knew a different Marvin, a Marvin grown weary and humor less with age. But Nellie, and maybe Linden, remembered a time when the three of them had camped out along the beach and searched for shells along the shore.

Hours later, a rattling sounded from outside, ending with a chugging that outlasted the sound of a motor. Nellie caught a glimpse of Linden's awful, rust-spotted van.

Lean and agile, Linden hadn't changed much from his hippie days. Same beard, same worn jeans. In his hand he carried a pale, white flower. "A sea lily," he said, extending it to her. Nellie's hands held the flower; Linden's hands held hers very tightly.

"Looks like you won the fight," he said with a droll, speculative glance at the black eye Nellie had received in the fall.

Jane glanced at John, so serious in their fear of hurting her feelings. They had never even mentioned her bruised and swollen eye.

Nellie had grown a little hard of hearing. She appreciated the way Linden took the time to speak distinctly without acting foolish or patronizing. Jane shouted when she spoke to Nellie, and John, because he never raised his voice, tended to leave her out of conversations entirely. It made her feel lost, forgotten, as if she were a ghost that people no longer saw or heard.

"The stairway won." Nellie smiled. Linden's presence always brightened her outlook, made even the taped ankle seem a little amusing. Even those old black shoes seemed less hideous as her mood lightened.

"A black eye adds character." Linden winked. "Shows the world you're not afraid."

"Linden," John's stiff formality broke into the lightness. "I need to have a word with you."

The voices began again, voices she could just barely make out, voices that sounded a little distant like the wind.

Gradually they grew louder; she caught some of what John was saying. "…can't stay here alone. I think Bill Martin will buy the house, so we've no real problems. We're taking Mother to Villa Rest tomorrow. Linden," he warned, "try not to upset her."

"Is that what she wants?"

"Do you think we haven't talked it over with her?"

"Then I want to see this wonderful place!" Linden said, turning to Nellie. "Mother, I want you to show me your room at Villa Rest."

John frowned. "She's already been out there once today."

"She really shouldn't be walking on that ankle yet," Jane chimed in.

Linden seemed not to hear them. "Do you want to go?"

"I'll go." Nellie reached for her crutch.

"She wants to go." Linden said firmly as he helped her from the chair. Outside the sunlight felt warm and comforting, so did Linden's arm as it supported her. Even though Nellie's ankle hurt when she tried to put any weight on it, she felt better.

How bored she had been day and night in confinement. The fall had dulled her senses, made it impossible for her to concentrate on her books or tend her flowerbeds. Now the petunias were brown and curled around the edges.

Linden picked her up and lifted her into the high van seat. "The easiest way," he laughed. "Besides, you've grown light as a feather." He lifted her out again when they arrived at Villa Rest. The two of them walked slowly toward the sleekly modern, brick building.

In the open recreation room, a group was playing cards. Linden stopped to talk to them. Something he said caused them all to laugh.

Linden really wasn't like her other children— every moment seemed so vital to him. Why, if he lived out here, Nellie thought, he would enjoy himself. Instead of just being so full of self-pity, she could try to be more like Linden.

"You'll have fun playing cards with that group," Linden chuckled. "But watch that one they call Skip!"

As they passed the TV, Linden said, "I forgot about the game. Who's winning?"

The old man's blank eyes never left the screen, which he seemed not even to see.

"This will be my room," Nellie said, leading Linden down the corridor, as white as the nurse's uniforms. The identical, impersonal rooms looked like rooms in a hospital. Nellie wondered if she would lose all sense of her individuality.

Nellie eased herself into the hard, high-backed chair and Linden rested upon the bed with its stiff pillows and thin, white cover. "What will you do here all day?"

"I can always read." Nellie knew that as long as she still had her eyesight, as long as there were books, she would not lose everything.

No Longer Drifting
Jackson-Britton

Linden, looking a little grim, stared out the window at the oak trees and well-mowed lawn. Nellie didn't like the view, the arena of silence, where she would have nothing to watch except the changing of the leaves.

The silence outside was magnified by the stillness within. For a long time neither of them spoke. Then Linden looked at her, his clear, blue eyes as stormy as a restless sea. "Is this really what you want?"

Nellie lifted her chin. "I won't be a burden to anyone. This place is nice. Very expensive. You know John. He insisted upon the top of the line."

"It would be okay." Linden shrugged. "If you really needed this kind of care. But I don't think you do. There's so much you haven't done or seen."

Nellie felt relieved to have someone talk to her as if she were still living. To Linden she could reveal her true thoughts, could be totally honest. "There comes a time when we must put other people's wishes first," she said sadly.

Her son's blue eyes locked into hers. "When we give our choices over to others, then we're...not free anymore. Isn't that right?"

Her oldest son, her failure. How could she answer such a question? How could she explain to him that John and Jane were both too successful to look after her? For an instant it flitted through her mind that

Linden—but, no, Linden couldn't look after her, either. Not with his passionate love for freedom. He could not think of burdening himself with an old woman!

Nellie's weariness increased as they drove back to the house. Using her throbbing ankle as an excuse, she told her children she was going to bed early. She had survived so many other crises. When Marvin had died, she had been more needed than ever before. But now—did she really have the courage or the will to survive this one? She closed her eyes with the deep and sincere wish that she would never have to open them again.

Early the next morning, Nellie found the house stripped bare. All of her personal belongings for the home were packed and waiting near the door. Boxes brimming with books, costume jewelry, statues and the little porcelain figures she had collected through the years were scattered around the room, ready to be received by Jane's charity.

Nellie wore her nicest dress, a silky print.

"Are you ready, Mother?"

Nellie's eyes misted. She tried to cover her trembling lips with a bright smile. "Ready as rain."

"I'll take her," Linden suddenly volunteered.

"It's hard for Mother to get into the van," John started to protest.

No Longer Drifting
Jackson-Britton

"We managed yesterday. Besides, you two have handled everything else. I want to do something."

Nellie saw John exchange a glance with Jane, then he spoke again, somewhat hesitantly, "I really should get back to the bank. I have a meeting at ten."

"The kids and I will come visit Saturday," Jane promised with a quick hug.

Linden grasped Nellie's large, brown suitcase and carried it to the van. When he came back, he looked around the room. "I want those books and a few other things," he said to Nellie.

"Of course you can have them." Nellie had seen where Jane had put her classics. "This box is the best."

"Give me a hand, John."

Nellie, settled in the front seat of the van, turned to wave at John and Jane. How hard it was for them. Why, Jane was starting to cry.

Nellie could not stop her own tears. No reason to stop them now.

The smell of the sea was in the van; she noticed the fine, sifted sand upon the floor. A longing to see the ocean again rushed over her. So many things she wanted to do just one more time!

At the crossroad, Linden stopped. With a twinkle in his eye, he asked, "Which way, Mother?"

"You know the way to Villa Rest. We were just out there yesterday."

No Longer Drifting
Jackson-Britton

A wave of his hand indicated opposing directions. "One way leads to Villa Rest, the other way leads to the sea. Which way do you really want to go?"

"What...what are you saying?"

"I'm saying I want you to come live with me."

"Is that *really* what you want?"

Linden's answer was a sudden turn onto the highway.

They had driven several miles before Nellie was able to believe it. Last night she had wanted to die, today Linden and she were happy, heading toward the ocean like a couple of adventurers. Her eyes fell to her feet, to the drab, old shoes she detested. "I won't be able to wear these shoes on the beach," she announced. "I'll need to buy some sandals." She hesitated, then added with decision, "Some white ones."

"Sandal shopping," Linden called, "next stop."

Nellie wondered for a moment what Jane or John would think when she called them and told them of her decision. It struck her as strange the way things sometimes turned out. John or Jane might have made room for her in their lives. But Linden...all of his life he had somehow evaded her sense of values, of responsibilities.

"Are you sure you want to do this, Linden? You—you're the one who's always wanted so much to be free."

No Longer Drifting
Jackson-Britton

"I am free!" Linden's white teeth gleamed in a gypsy smile. "I'll always be free...to do the things I really want to do."

No Longer Drifting
Jackson-Britton

Two young girls left alone must make a painful decision.

AN ACT OF MERCY

Warm spring rain brought a bountiful supply of tomatoes, berries, and weeds to our garden. Mama left early this morning to spend time with Timmy and his wife and the new baby, leaving my big sister, Esther, in charge. Gardening was a job Esther loved. I watched her strong, tanned hands with their thick, slightly callused palms work the hoe, methodically chopping at the weeds near the edge of the strawberry patch.

The afternoon sunlight was lazy and warm. I bit into a ripe strawberry, tasting the sweetness, licking the juice from sticky fingers. I was seven years old and on days like this the world seemed full of butterflies, life, and promise. I was content to follow along beside Esther, watching her work, sometimes wandering off to explore the tangle of weeds beyond the tomato vines. At the edge of the garden was a forest playground of root and thistle still undisturbed by Esther's hoe.

Just beyond the last thorny row of gooseberry bushes, I spotted a small hole in the ground. I squatted down to peer inside, and that's when I saw them. Tiny rabbits! "Esther, look!" I cried out in delight. But she was too busy to hear me, or even turn around.

I crawled closer, moving the thin layer of leaves and brambles. Three of them were hiding in the little hole. Eagerly, I reached my hands inside, taking out one, then another, until all of them huddled in the lap of my flowered skirt, pink noses quivering, frightened eyes blinking in the bright afternoon sun.

A shadow suddenly stood over me. It was Esther. "Oh, Mary!" I heard my sister's cry of dismay as she stared down at the baby rabbits in my lap. "What have you done?"

"I'm just playing with them." I glanced up at her, confused by her reaction. She was not pleased and happy as I thought she would be, but seemed upset with me, almost angry. "I just love little things," I said. "You know I wouldn't do them any harm."

No Longer Drifting
Jackson-Britton

The dying sunlight slanted warm rays across the garden. I saw beads of sweat on Esther's forehead as she pushed back damp locks of hair that had escaped her thick braid. "You should never touch baby rabbits," she scolded. "Now, when the mother comes back, she won't recognize her own babies. When she smells the scent of human on them, she will reject them." Esther's voice lowered slightly, her deep-set hazel eyes avoiding mine. "Without their mother to feed them, they will starve."

"Oh, no!" I looked down at the warm little balls of white fur that I had impulsively taken from the rabbit's nest and unwittingly sealed their fate. Guilt gnawed at my stomach. "What if I put them right back?"

Esther shook her head. "It's too late now."

"Then what are we going to do with them?" I looked up at her hopefully. "Maybe we could keep them for pets."

Esther bent down to examine one of the little creatures. A deep frown creased her tanned forehead. "I'm afraid they're too young to wean. They wouldn't live."

The sun was going down. The warmth of the day rapidly disappeared, leaving a chill in my heart. "Then what are we going to do?"

I saw Esther's gaze move toward the hoe. "We're going to have to kill them."

No Longer Drifting
Jackson-Britton

"No!" Desperate tears filled my eyes. "I—I wish Mama was here!" Mama would know what to do. But she was far away taking care of our brother's wife and the new baby.

"Mama would do the same thing," Esther insisted. "I've seen her do it time and again with gophers and rabbits. Whenever she accidentally disturbs a wild animal's nest she takes the hoe..."

Esther reached for the sharp-bladed instrument.

I cradled the bunnies protectively in my lap. "I won't let you kill them like that!"

I saw her hesitate. Her face seemed gray in the fading sunlight. She looked dusty and tired after the long day in the sun. Her eyes darted here and there, frightened like the rabbits.

"Bring them around to the back porch," she said finally.

Not knowing what else to do, I silently obeyed. "Watch them. Don't let them get away."

The bunnies were beginning to grow braver and more restless. Even as small as they were, they could hop and buck, and there was a surprising strength in the tiny legs. I put them on the old dog's blanket in the corner. Esther went into the house. She returned with a wooden mop bucket and began to fill it with water from the pump near the edge of the porch.

Fear for the rabbits made my throat tight. I could

feel a terrible pounding in my head. "What are you going to do?"

"I'm going to have to drown them."

I tried to grab the bucket from her. Water sloshed upon the floor. "No!" My voice rose in panic. I won't let you!"

"It has to be done, Mary," she insisted, shaking off my hands with some of Mama's iron-clad firmness. "Look at them! They're helpless. They don't have a chance. If we set them free, some coyote will get them. At least this way it'll be over quick. I promise you they won't suffer."

Tears blurred my eyes as I forced myself to look at the wild little creatures that, in my innocence, I had condemned to death. Our raised voices had frightened them. They were still now, huddled together in a furry mass upon the old dog's blanket. I thought about scooping them up in my arms and running with them. But what would I do with them? How could I keep them alive?

"Maybe you'd better go into the house."

Defiant, I stood between Esther and the rabbits. "You can't make me!"

"Go into the house." Her voice was menacing, quiet, like Mama's was when I did something especially bad. Esther was a head taller than me. She could still get the better of me in a fight. When she took another threatening step toward me I knew my cause was lost.

"I hate you!" I cried. "I'll never forgive you!" I ran into the house, slamming the door hard behind me. How could anyone be so heartless and cruel? And yet I had seen the look of dread in my sister's eyes. In my heart, I knew that drowning the rabbits was a task Esther felt had to be done, not something that she wanted to do.

I went up to my room and buried my face in the soft feather pillow. I think I must have fallen asleep, at least for a little while. When I opened my eyes, the sun had gone down, and the air was cool.

My stomach ached, but I wasn't sure why. Then, with a sick feeling, I remembered Esther and the rabbits. The memory jolted me into wakefulness. I hurried back out to the porch. In the twilight, I saw Esther sitting on the floor beside the wooden bucket. The rabbits were gone.

I glanced from the bucket to the slippery trail of water that led to the end of the porch. I turned back to my sister, noticing for the first time that her skirt and sleeves were soaked. "They fought me," she said. "I--I couldn't do it."

I could barely believe my ears. "What—"

"I turned them loose."

She covered her face with her hands. "They're all wet," she cried. "And it's getting colder. They'll freeze to death now." She sniffled. "They're worse off than if I'd have left them alone."

I looked outside, but the babies were nowhere to be seen. I thought about the rabbits, my rabbits, hiding cold and wet and alone out there in the brush, easy prey to the hungry bobcats and coyotes.

"Don't cry, Sis," I said, putting my arms around her and hugging her close. "Maybe you washed our scent off. Maybe the mother will know her babies now, after all. I'll bet she'll find them and put them right back in their nest. I just know she will!"

Hope returned to Esther's voice. "Do you really think so?" I could feel the dampness of her sleeves as her arms came around my neck, holding me tight. I don't know why I felt such love for my sister that day; did I feel sorriest for her because she had tried to drown my rabbits in the first place, or because, in the end, she had let them go?

Dara resented deeply the suffocating role marriage had placed upon her. Was there any way out?

DO YOU TAKE…?

Dara drove across Texas toward the Gulf of Mexico. She needed to get away, to be by herself, to think about one thing mainly: whether or not she would return.

A loveless marriage—she had committed herself to it, had lit candles on anniversaries like some worshiping priest—an act by which commitment became tangible. Tangibility became the substance, representing nothing.

Gerald had allowed her to go alone, as if he believed her story about visiting Tina. "I had the van tuned," he had said. "Don't forget to check the oil. It's beginning to use oil." Responsibility added to responsibility marred the edges of his mouth, placed deep creases around his eyes, so quick to see what must be done. Over the years he had developed a manner of studied compromise between caution and action. Or had he always been like that, even as a boy, sitting across the aisle from her at Harden High School?

"I'll take care of the van."

"Tell Tina to come see us. It's such a shock about Jim. Just one moment of carelessness..." He snapped his fingers instead of finishing. "You drive carefully."

"Sure. Tell Billy..." She had driven off without completing her sentence. Later she tried to finish the sentence as she drove along. Tell Billy I stayed only because of him. Now that he's grown and living in the dorm, tell him I'm not coming back.

Dara had packed everything she would need. Their camping gear was always in the van, and money—they never quarreled about money. Gerald worked hard. They had plenty of it. She had withdrawn from her savings account and had tucked the thick stack of travelers' checks into her suitcase.

And here she was on Highway 281 south of San Antonio. Why didn't she feel free?

Once she had eagerly accepted change and challenge. That's when singing had been her whole life, when she was being asked more and more often to appear in shows and on local TV stations. Somewhere in the cooking, the scrubbing, the teaching of Billy, her dreams had fallen. Now her chance was gone. A few opportunities not taken and there it was—all behind her.

Once the whole world had lain like an open road full of promise. The road stretching before her now was filled with the agony of not knowing, the despair of having never found.

When Dara reached Corpus Christi, she headed for the sea-side park where Gerald and she used to fish from the pier. Maybe she only needed time alone, days spent walking by the ocean.

"How many in your party?" asked the ranger.

How could she bear being alone? She couldn't even say the number. "Two."

"Stay on the blacktop," he said. "The sand is for tenters."

* * *

She met Quentin on the fourth day of June, her second full day at the beach. Back from a long, exhausting jog, Dara found a dilapidated pickup truck edged very close beside the van. A tall man, shirtless, way too thin in baggy, frayed shorts, was trying to start a fire in the grate, but the strong, ocean breeze squelched each attempt.

No Longer Drifting
Jackson-Britton

She answered his, "Hello, neighbor!" with a prim, "Hi," and hurried off to the shower-room to change from her swimming suit into a sweat suit. She paused before the mirror. Nothing she could do with her hair, she decided; just let it string long, dark, straight, around her face. Gerald always wanted her to cut it. He wanted her to look like Mrs. Chairman-of-the-Board; a wife styled to complement his vice-presidency.

When she got back to camp, she set out the camp stove and began frying the small fish she had caught early this morning. She tried not to glance at her neighbor, but she could feel his eyes behind dark sunglasses watching her.

"Smells good," he said at last.

She cast a quick look at him then. He wasn't husky or immaculate like Gerald, but slender, small-framed, free, just as she had always wanted to be, like the lone gulls that soared above and that settled nowhere for long.

He took off the sunglasses. The deep suntan brought attention to his eyes, blue-green and so very clear, like tropical water. She envied at once his air of contentment. She liked his swift, unselfconscious gestures, the way he brought a hand up to sweep back the limp, black hair. Her reply was a constrained, tight smile.

No Longer Drifting
Jackson-Britton

"Baked beans. Potato chips." He lifted items from a sack sitting on the tailgate of his truck as he spoke. "We could join forces. Unless you're expecting your husband back or someone."

"No one," she said. "There's a plastic cloth in the back of the van if you want to set the table."

As they began eating, gulls arrived, one by one, standing at a distance, watching. Occasionally one would fly above them, suspended, screaming for notice.

Quentin told her he was from Port Aransas, that he worked only part-time for Ron's Deep Sea Fishing. "I only want money enough to support my loafing," he said.

She laughed at almost everything he said, at the enthusiastic way he pitched leftovers to the waiting gulls.

"Are you...married?" she asked him.

The smile that lined his face even when he was serious intensified at her question. "I make no commitments," he answered. "And you?"

"I make them," she said, then added, "and try to avoid them."

That wasn't entirely truthful, she thought, as she lay that night in her bed in back of the van. Dara resented deeply the suffocating role marriage had placed upon her, but she had been a faithful wife, a star mother, a perfect sister to Tina, whom she should be visiting now. Poor Tina, only four months ago Jim had died because of that foolish accident.

Quentin had dragged an old army cot from the pickup and placing his head against the side of the truck to shield himself from the strong ocean wind, lay looking up at the stars. She didn't lock the door of the van. She felt safe with him. He seemed to believe in perfect freedom for everyone.

In the morning, Dara rose early. She wanted to be the first one on the beach as the ocean receded. The salty air was invigorating. Her long hair blew freely. She felt the tugging of the tide as it displaced the sand around her feet as she walked.

After a while she left the water to examine the scattering of seaweed and shells left behind on the shore.

"You missed one!"

Dara looked behind her and saw Quentin lift a perfect shell from the harsh, moving water.

He was interested in everything they found. He had to take off his shirt to use for a sack and it was completely full when they returned to camp. They sat drinking coffee and inspecting their treasures.

"This," he held up a streaked, sea-encrusted bottle, "was probably cast from some China-freighter! It could tell exciting stories of great adventure on the high seas!"

No Longer Drifting
Jackson-Britton

"It was probably left from a beach party."

He set the bottle between them, waving thin hands over it. "Speak to us, sea bottle. What story do you tell?"

Dara, ready with a quip, was stopped by a hand indicating silence.

"Hush. The great bottle speaks. It is saying 'this great treasure you have found together.' Quentin's unsmiling face seemed still to smile as he regarded the bottle with absorbed attention.

"What else does it say?"

"It says, 'You must take good care of me'."

* * *

Dara phoned Tina the next day.

"Gerald has been calling constantly," Tina said. "He thought you'd be here by now. He's worried sick."

"Tell him I'll call. Soon."

"Where are you? When will you be here?"

"I'm Ok, Tina," Dara cut her short. "I'll call you Saturday."

Saturday! Three wonderful days to spend on the beach with Quentin!

Friday night Quentin slept with her in the van. He made love to her with great passion. He wasn't tender, considerate, anxious to please her, the way Gerald was. His body felt wiry and strange against hers, not natural or good. Afterwards she didn't want to remain in his arms, the way she always did with Gerald. Maybe it was because she had never made love to anyone but Gerald. Maybe that's why she felt dirty, guilty, more alone than she had ever felt before.

Quentin was soon asleep—a stranger, whose slight snoring disturbed her. She lay awake thinking of Billy, of Tina, and of Gerald. It was almost dawn before she fell asleep.

"You're going to miss tide-out!" Quentin spoke, opening the door, as if the van were his.

Dara sat up wondering where she was, who he was. When she remembered, she wanted to cry.

She busied herself with routine, frying bacon, breaking eggs into the skillet. After breakfast she began packing the van.

"You're not leaving, are you? You said you'd be here several days."

"I've changed my mind," she answered. As she washed the dishes and packed them into the picnic basket, she told him about her life, about Gerald.

He accepted her revelation with a silence that seemed to ignore her plight, her pain. "Let's go down to the beach," he spoke at last.

"I'd better get an early start."

"Your sister isn't even expecting you today. An hour or two won't make any difference."

No Longer Drifting
Jackson-Britton

She arranged and rearranged the load while Quentin stood by every once and a while saying, "What's your hurry?" or "Why not one more swim?"

Dara had intended to just drive away, but her spending the morning here seemed so important to him, and what difference did it make to her?

They had fun swimming. She was by far the better swimmer. He kept calling for her not to go out too far. When they tired of swimming, they built sand castles. She even sang for him some of the old songs she used to sing.

"You should be on stage," he told her.

* * *

Later they climbed into the old truck and drove for miles and miles along the sandy shoreline. The gray, overcast skies hinted of an approaching storm, but the air sweeping in through the open windows was deliciously warm and left a moist, salty film on their lips.

Groups of swimmers became fewer. At last they encountered only isolation. Quentin pulled the truck to a sudden stop near the remains of an old rock pier that jutted out into the water. He jumped out, shouting, "Today you learn to surf!"

She might have known he was still a surfer. How many years had he spent here with the wind and water? He would have to be as old as Gerald but he was still a boy. "Not me!" she informed him. "Not today. Those waves look terrible!"

"Just right for surfing!" He laughed. "Coward! Come on!"

"No, I'll watch."

"You'll miss the fun!'

"Maybe after while. I'll just watch."

Surfboard in hand, Quentin ran head-on into the great waves. Dara entertained herself hunting for shells. Ever so often, she glanced toward Quentin, admiring the skillful poise of his thin body, the agile way he stayed on top of the board.

His form now seemed distant. She could barely hear his yelling, "Now watch this!"

She stopped walking to watch. He reminded her of Billy a few years back and she smiled.

The wave he rode was frighteningly high. It seemed angled too far north, toward the jutting rocks of the pier.

"Be careful!" she shouted into the wind. "Quentin, be careful!"

The gigantic wave seemed to rise in protest, like some raging, rodeo bull. It tore the surfboard out from under his feet and hurled him off as if he were weightless. Dara watched helplessly as Quentin slammed against jagged rocks. Then she saw only the wild, rolling water, gray and angry, and the lone, red surfboard floating and bobbing and rocking first one way, then another.

Dara heard her own scream as she raced, meeting the furious waves with a force she didn't know she possessed. Once she stopped, tried to touch the bottom, but couldn't. Quentin had just disappeared into the vast, churning water. How would she ever find him?

Again and again she dived beneath waves, unmindful of the thick, salty liquid she sucked into her lungs. Her eyes burned and seemed unable to focus. She fought, half-blinded. A wave smacked against her, tossing her back toward the shore. Dara battled it with all the strength of mind and body.

She saw first the back of his head, the limp, black hair spreading out in every direction. She reached out to grasp the hair. She tugged him toward her, locking her left arm around his neck. It was useless to try to hold his head above the high, shifting water. She didn't even try. She struggled, working with the waves that now propelled them toward the shore.

Dara dragged Quentin to the dry sand away from the water, and stood over him, choking, coughing up seawater and half-crying. He was badly injured. Blood seeped from an open gap low on his back. She dreaded to touch him, but knew if she didn't, he would have no chance at all.

No Longer Drifting
Jackson-Britton

She turned his head to the side and tried desperately to recall what she had seen so long ago in a first-aid class. She located what she thought was the right position and pressed hard below the ribs of his back. She counted carefully: one, two, three; one, two three.

Water ran freely from Quentin's mouth at each thrust of her hands. Be steady. Be calm! One, two, three.

Finally she noticed a motion of his head, heard a strangled sound like a cough. She did not let up. She continued working with him, on and on, until she was absolutely certain he was breathing on his own. Thank God!

She fell beside him, exhausted. "I'm afraid to move you!" she said, her voice hoarse, far away. "I'm going to drive back to the ranger station and get help."

* * *

As Dara waited for the men to load Quentin into the ambulance, she found in his truck a pair of jeans and an old shirt to slip on over her bathing suit. She climbed in the ambulance beside him.

She tried to hear his words above the screeching siren. At last she made out one word. "Agnes!"

Dara bent closer.

"Agnes. My legs. They're so cold!"

No Longer Drifting
Jackson-Britton

Dara stood back while attendants transported Quentin into the emergency room, then she followed. In a short time a doctor came out of the examining room. She rose to her feet, a sinking in her stomach as she read the expression on his face.

"A back injury. It could be very serious. Are you his wife?"

"No."

"He's in shock. We're treating him now for that. If he had got here a minute or two later, we wouldn't be treating him for anything." He turned to the nurse. "You must contact next of kin right away. We need a go-ahead to operate."

* * *

"I'm Agnes Brewer," said the small, blonde woman to the nurse at the desk. "Quentin Brewer's wife."

Dara could see her through the doorway. She looked so fragile, small-boned; pretty, in a faded, sad sort of way. Trying hard to be composed, she spoke quietly to the young doctor, then the older one who had talked to Dara. When they left, she moved woodenly into the waiting room and sat down directly across from Dara. She looked frightened and faint.

"May I get you some coffee?" Dara asked.

Agnes' hand shook as she accepted the paper cup. She started to bring it to her lips, but didn't drink, just set it aside.

No Longer Drifting
Jackson-Britton

In the quietness Dara listened to the footsteps of nurses, to the constant ringing of phones.

"You were the one who found him." Agnes spoke hollowly.

It didn't sound like a question, still Dara answered. "Yes."

Agnes' gaze lingered on her, made Dara feel as if she were made of glass. Shadows had moved into Agnes' pale eyes. The shadows made Dara uneasy.

Were Quentin's transgressions so common? Agnes' whole life must have been spent in acceptance and resignation. Dara was certain she knew the truth. Then why was she pretending she didn't know? Her silence was worse than confrontation!

Dara backed away toward the window. She felt tears forming behind her eyes, so thick she could hardly see. She felt tears appearing as a sharp pain in her throat. Why did this have to happen? What if Quentin died? Why hadn't he told her about Agnes?

Cold, deep silence, like ocean waves, washed over her. Silence remained with them throughout the hours they waited, until, at last, the doctor returned and gestured to Agnes from the doorway.

The aging doctor and Agnes talked near the admission's desk where Dara could see them. Dara heard the last of his sentence. "...best thing for you to do is go on home."

No Longer Drifting
Jackson-Britton

"I'm not leaving. I'm going to stay here."

Dara's gaze locked on Agnes' face. The dark smudges beneath her eyes intensified what was fragile, what was tragic.

Agnes collapsed into the chair, eyes closed tightly. Wet strands of pale hair clung to her forehead. Dara bent closer to hear her words. "My prayers have been answered."

The sob, that for hours had been forming, escaped Dara's throat—relief, gratitude. "What did the doctor say?"

"He said Quentin will recover. There'll be no permanent damage to his legs or back."

* * *

All night long at the beach the wind blew sand across the cement slabs of the camping area. Dara watched it swirl, settle momentarily, then rise and shift. She lay awake wondering if her life from here on would drift in a similar manner.

Dara left the campground early the next morning. Wanting to be certain of Quentin's condition before she left Corpus Christi, she stopped by the hospital.

"Saver of lives," he said as she entered his room. The color had returned to his skin, bronze surrounding white. "Don't tell me," he said. "You're leaving. Going back to Gerald."

She shook her head. "I'm going to stay with my sister for a while. Sort things out."

Their conversation, void of the easy exchange that had once marked it, was filled with hesitation. Dara forced into uncomfortable periods of silence commonplace remarks—how strong the wind had blown last night; how vacant the beach was this morning. "You'll be back out there in no time," she added.

"I'm always at the beach," Quentin said, and he reminded her of it again before she left.

The corridor was empty except for a nurse at the desk reading a chart. Agnes appeared from around the corner, smiling anxiously and greeting her as if they were old companions. "He's getting along so well!" she said. Her delicate features were still marked by a look of fear and shock.

Dara understood her suffering and felt stirrings of anger against Quentin. His great freedom seemed to be purchased at his wife's expense. He was trying to find happiness by avoiding responsibility. How childish! How impossible!

"Quentin looks fine, doesn't he?"

"Yes," Dara answered. "He'll soon be surfing again."

Before getting on the elevator, Dara turned back to watch Agnes hurry toward Quentin's room. How much Quentin took from her, Dara thought. How little he gave! Poor Agnes.

* * *

As Dara left the hospital, her sympathy extended to include Gerald.

On a frantic trip through the desert, a childish game goes wrong.

TROLLS

"Are there really trolls out here?" five-year-old Benjamin asked from the back seat as Cindy drove the winding stretch of road toward Tonopah, Nevada. She glanced at her son in the old Impala's rearview mirror. His reflection, eyes brown and trusting in his thin, earnest face, stared back at her. His T-shirt needed washing. Ben clutched his favorite stuffed toy, a worn rabbit, to his chest.

"Sure. Can't you see them hiding behind the rocks?" Her reply came automatically as Cindy drove along, lost in thought, battling the monotony of the deserted highway, hoping the gas needle wouldn't dip much lower until they reached the next town.

Her shoulders ached and her eyes felt grainy from driving all afternoon. Slightly overweight, she did not take the heat well. Beads of perspiration formed on her lips and her damp blonde hair felt flattened against her scalp.

The harsh glare of the setting sun struck the windshield, half-blinding her, making it difficult to see the many twists and curves. Squinting against the light gave her a splitting headache.

Not another car in sight. The map she had found in the dash compartment touted Highway 6 as the "loneliest road in the United States," and Cindy was beginning to believe it. The ribbon of rough asphalt wound its way around monolithic cliffs interspersed by wide, flat areas where granite boulders set as if they had been dropped by some giant hand in the sky onto barren fields of sagebrush.

"Look, Mommy. I think I see one!" Ben's voice was high with enthusiasm.

Troll-watching… a game she had made up fifty miles ago to keep her active son occupied. It had worked all too well. For more than half an hour he had kept his eyes trained from the window, searching for some sign of purple or green hair, a face half-concealed behind rock.

"Mommy! I think I see another one."

"Um humm," Cindy replied.

"You didn't really look, and now you've missed him," Ben accused fretfully.

The game she had invented as a distraction was rapidly becoming an annoyance. "I'll catch the next one, Benny. Promise."

"Maybe there won't be any more." Ben pouted.

Silence fell again. Cindy's mind drifted back to the night before, when Duane in a drunken stupor had not even noticed their quiet escape. While he snored, open-mouthed, an empty bottle of Jack Daniels cradled in his arm, she had bundled Benjamin and their meager belongings into the car. Cindy had driven clear from San Diego, California, crossing the state line before she had stopped and pulled off at the side of the road for a few hours sleep. She was desperate to put as much distance as she could between them before Duane awoke and found them gone.

She had driven steadily except for a couple of hasty stops at the few gas stations and shabby roadside diners along the way. She thought she had caught sight of a red Mustang in the parking lot just outside the cafe where they had eaten breakfast. She told herself it was only her imagination, he couldn't have picked up their trail so quickly. Still, her nerves had become more and more frazzled and since then she had stopped only for gas, getting back on the road again as quickly as possible.

"Are the trolls nice or mean, Mommy?" She glanced back at Ben. He had been working his way through a bag of chocolate chip cookies she had bought at the last gas station and his sticky fingers left dark smudges on the stuffed rabbit's gray ears.

"Only nice ones live out here."

The old car's engine began to sputter. *If it stalled out on her, if he found them alone in this deserted place...Dear God, Cindy prayed. Don't let it stall!* The engine coughed and then began to run smoothly again. Still, the desperate feeling would not leave the pit of her stomach. She had a hundred and fifty dollars left in her purse. Not nearly enough to start over. Not nearly enough to begin a new life.

"In my storybooks trolls are mean," Ben persisted. "They eat people."

"Not these trolls," Cindy repeated. "These trolls are nice."

She had reached a long, straight stretch of road. When she got to the next town, Tonopah, Cindy would look up her only living relative, an aunt she hadn't seen since she was a child. Maybe Aunt Minnie would take them in for a while. Just until she could start applying for jobs and find a place to live. Surely

No Longer Drifting
Jackson-Britton

Duane would never find them way out here, in the middle of nowhere!

A maid's job, a cook's job was all she could hope for. Anything to temporarily put food on the table, while she looked for something better. If she could only have foreseen the future, she would have finished high school and waited before jumping into marriage. It had started out so good and gone so wrong! Duane— slowly rotting his mind on hard liquor and dope. The only good thing that had come of their marriage was Ben.

"I saw another one." Benjamin's voice was high, frightened. "He didn't look very nice. He had lots of teeth. Big ones."

"Only your imagination, Bennie-Bear," she replied automatically, her gaze never straying from the endless gray ribbon of road, which now curved snake-like around the tan, barren hills.

"How do you know, you didn't look. You didn't even see him, did you, Mommy?" His little voice was accusing. "Did you, Mommy?"

Lost in her own thoughts, she didn't answer. Soon, all was quiet from the back seat. Ben must have fallen asleep. Cindy was grateful for the silence. The isolation of the road once again began to hypnotize her. Cindy settled back into her endless cycle of thought, a place to live, a job, any job, then think about school. Don't think about Duane. Don't think about him at all. Going back to him was no longer an option.

"I'll never let you take Ben," Duane had vowed. "If I can't have him, you won't either. If you ever leave me, I'll come after you," he had warned. "And I'll hurt both of you!" Her arm was bruised where he had gripped it, but at least he hadn't beat her this time...at least he hadn't laid a hand on Ben! His drunken words, the threat in his eyes still made Cindy shudder. She knew the kind of violence Ben was capable of, the irrational turn of his thoughts.

A piercing shriek tore from the back seat. "Trolls! Trolls!" Small, sticky hands clamped around the base of her neck. Ben must have awakened from a nightmare. The sudden noise after so much silence, after her thoughts of Duane, made Cindy start.

"Stop it, Ben!" She pulled his hands away. Too late! In the moment she had taken to turn her head Cindy missed a curve in the road, felt herself skid, applied the brakes.

The Impala hit a bump, then like a horse bolting free from a stable, began to careen wildly away from the road, then came to a screeching halt on the sandy shoulder.

"Look what you've done "Cindy cried, shaken. "You almost made me wreck!"

"The trolls. They are following us. They want to kill us and eat us all up!"

She turned to see Ben huddled in the back seat, curled into a little ball, terrified by his fantasy fears. Why had she ever made up this foolish game? She rubbed her aching head. "Listen to me, Ben. There are no trolls, okay? It's a game. Just a silly, stupid game."

Ben, unconvinced, continued to whimper, his hands covering his face.

"Come up here with me." Cindy lifted her arms to help Ben climb over the seat, helped him fasten his seat belt. He huddled close to her. She cranked the engine, sighed with relief when it once more sputtered to life. Keeping one arm protectively around Ben's thin shoulder, she continued to drive.

"Honey, there aren't any trolls. And even if there were, don't you know I would never, ever, let them or anything else harm you?"

Slowly, he relaxed against her and his sobbing ceased. Soon, he was fast asleep. Cindy glanced at him beside her, so small, so vulnerable, then trained her eyes back to the road, to the weathered sign up ahead which read Tonopah. Duane's words echoed in her mind, *"Wherever you go, whatever you do, I'll find you, find you, find you..."*

No Longer Drifting
Jackson-Britton

Cindy drew in her breath, knowing that the real danger lurked not in the hills around them but in the curve around the next bend, and the ever-present threat of tomorrow.

Cathy sensed the cold darkness that was a part of Winston Kincade, yet she felt helpless, unable to break away.

THE BLAMELESS

From out of all the people at the crowded party, why did his eyes, dark and luminous, seek mine? I could no more avert my gaze than I could stop breathing. From that first moment I became his victim, to be stalked like a lion stalks prey in the interior of some dark, wild jungle. One fact, clear and certain, consoles me yet: I am not now and never was a part of his evil plans.

"See that man talking to Mr. Moore?" My girlhood friend and business assistant, April Stenson, shook my sleeve as if she were some giddy schoolgirl. "Have you ever seen anyone so dreamily handsome? Doesn't he just take your breath away?"

"Leave it to you to spot the cute ones."

"As if you didn't!" April giggled, exactly as she had done eleven years ago at our high school prom. She leaned closer and spoke confidentially, "I'd say he's interested in you. Very, very, interested!"

Instead of joining April in her girlish delight, I felt a prompting to take refuge, as if I were already aware of some imposing threat rising to destroy my safe, well-ordered life. But my body did not obey my will and kept me in direct line with what I understood at once to be danger. I had immediately fallen under the spell of his unsettling self-assurance, the irresistible force of a man who will not be turned away from what he wants.

"Cathy, what are you doing?" April cried, bright, long-nailed fingers digging into my wrist. "You can't just leave! They're coming over." Even as she spoke, our boss and the towering stranger were walking toward us.

I braced myself. What on earth was wrong with me? I would have expected such a foolish fluttering of the heart to be experienced by someone like April, innocent and gullible, for all her red-hair tinting and thick mascara. Despite her attempts at worldliness she would never be more than a girl. I couldn't remember ever being that naive.

No Longer Drifting
Jackson-Britton

Alone--but I had never considered myself vulnerable. An unfortunate marriage, early dashed to bits, had left me satisfied with solitude, content to assume full control. The diversion, the trivia, that made up other people's lives, I had ruthlessly cut from my own--the result: vice-presidency of Branden-Moore Publications before the age of thirty, with only one man, the aging Luther Moore, between me and my life's ambition--full, complete authority.

"Wait, Cathy," Luther Moore's deep voice prohibited my fearful retreat. Around his lively, blue eyes deep smile lines crinkled. "There is someone I want you to meet. This is Winston Kincade. He has spent the entire evening trying to sell me on the idea that he would be a great asset to our firm and will not believe that we have no available openings. His persistence is wearying me. It may take you, Cathy, to convince him."

Woodenly I offered up my hand to be locked long and tightly in his steel-like grasp.

"Catherine Kelly," I informed him somewhat coldly.

"My second in command," Luther Moore added with pride.

"Kelly, is it?" Winston Kincade's smile revealed strong, very white teeth. "An Irish rose adrift in a sea of paper!"

No Longer Drifting
Jackson-Britton

His reference to my being adrift sparked my resentment. I had never been considered a person without direction. I tried to smile, as April and Luther Moore did, at his half-teasing compliment, but my attempt was at most weak, intimidated by his imposing presence. This man possessed remarkable power, power that went beyond the physical--the all-consuming force of a cunning and ambitious mind. The chilling essence of Winston Kincade I alone recognized; the others were taken in by the soulfulness of his large, dark eyes.

For over a week in my huge, plush office just down the corridor from Luther Moore's, I staunchly refused all calls from Winston Kincade. Each time I answered April's questioning gaze as she waited, receiver close to her lips, with increasing urgency. "Tell him I'm not in!"

"Ms. Kelly is in conference," April's formal voice announced. "May I take a message?"

"Tell Ms. Kelly I will call again. And again."

April replaced the receiver. Her birdlike appraisal had grown perplexed. "You must be..." she slowly spelled out the word, "c-r-a-z-y!"

When he had not called for several days, I began to breathe easier. The storm would soon abate and leave me quite the same. I left the office Friday evening after a board meeting that had dragged endlessly. To soothe the tension of long hours of pointless talk, I decided to walk the three blocks to my apartment.

The dim, gray sky, filled with a fine mist, saddened me. Everyone strolled in twos, in families, in groups. Aloneness exposes, places a person in a defenseless position, sets him or her apart. I wished I had accepted April's offer to join her at the club.

As I shifted my briefcase, crammed with manuscripts, and fumbled with my door key, I became aware of a looming form behind me. I whirled around.

Winston Kincade gave a slight bow, extended a pretty, cloth shamrock of the brightest green. "Call in sick in the morning!" he said in a voice full of authority. "Tomorrow will be ours! We will go to the St. Patrick's Day Parade, dance, eat cake with green frosting!"

"I don't think..." My voice trailed off. For countless years I had denied myself all pursuit of simple pleasures. Why shouldn't I have one, single day? How could I decline, when he looked so like a star in some sophisticated romance—damp black hair falling forward as he ducked his head and gave me such an appealing smile.

"I'll call for you at eight a.m."

That St. Patrick's Day I will never forget. Winston broke into the parade, dragging me with him, and we, waving, laughing, holding hands, marched down the street in front of the masses of people. Afterwards we stuffed ourselves with Irish stew, hard-tack biscuits, and pastries with sticky, green icing. We danced to lively jigs until my feet ached. After experiencing that long, beautiful day of freedom, I had no heart to deny him anything.

Had I not been so enamored with him, I would have found much to dislike in the changes that came over my neat apartment the moment he moved in. He rigidly enforced disorder, not allowing me to hang up his clothes, or move even slightly his books and papers. Moreover, he sneaked in a great shaggy cur named Girard, who scratched fleas and defied me on the grounds of his enormous size.

Almost every evening I would find Winston working on the computer he had set up on my kitchen table. "Launching my career," he would say when I made inquiries about his seemingly useless labor.

Many an evening I found myself still alone, save for Girard, who never tired of battling me over a place of comfort on the couch, where I once had peacefully read alone.

I no longer had any safe-haven, all my own. I should have out and out ordered him to leave my house, but I didn't.

A month later, out of the blue, Winston announced, "I cannot find work here. I am going to have to move on, maybe go back to Frisco."

No Longer Drifting
Jackson-Britton

I felt a pitiful sinking of heart. In some crazy, hypnotic way, Winston had become essential. Like a losing gambler, even though the game opposed to my own good, I found it totally impossible to forsake. "I didn't know…work…meant so much to you."

"I will not be a shiftless bum, living off a woman!" he declared vehemently. "My mind is made up."

I hesitated. "Let me talk to Mr. Moore. Maybe if I ask him, he will find a place for you in the office."

Despite Winston's sterling qualifications--he had worked for an international publishing company in the east--I knew the conservative Luther Moore would make no opening for another employee. Actually, I was faced with only one alternative--April. I could replace April, lose my girlhood friend instead of Winston, and make him my assistant.

Much suffering on my part brought this about. Several times I wandered away from the carved, leaded-glass door with the painted letters: Luther Moore, President, Branden-Moore Publications, quite willing to give it up. But at last I found myself facing the thin, white-haired man across his huge desk and saying with great reluctance, "A very serious matter has arisen. I must discuss it with you."

Luther Moore, friend much more than boss, had been from the first my mentor, quick to praise, to teach, to promote. I had the greatest respect for him and wished I did not have to go through with this.

"Of course, Cathy. Make yourself comfortable."

I gazed behind him where a picture of his partner, the bearded Fred Branden, many years dead, tranquilly smiled. Scrawled across his massive stomach in huge letters, he had written: To Luther, Who combines ambition with character.

The leather chair, richly cushioned, suddenly felt rigid and cold.

"I've been worried for a long time about April's work," I blurted out. Even as I spoke, images flashed before my eyes of two little girls playing doll, building sand castles, scribbling on posters. In spite of the variety and unstableness of her many pursuits, April did take a serious approach to her work and in all truth I had no complaint with her. But what other choice did I have? "She is my best friend," I spoke. "I'm at the point of not knowing what to do."

Luther Moore slumped back in his chair. Light from the window fell across his aristocratic features, made them as pale as marble. He did not speak for such a long time that I began to grow worried. Luther Moore never failed to show forth high principles, had himself made Branden-Moore a publishing company of the highest standards, of the most respected reputation. The few people he singled out to trust, he assumed possessed each of his forthright qualities. At the same time, he was perceptive--could it be that he guessed my motives? Did he detect about my bearing evidence of deception?

"I've always had the greatest admiration for you, Cathy," he said at last. "I think I admire you all the more for coming to me with this problem. You see, I know just how much April means to you. You must find this very painful."

"I feel I can't go on the way things are now."

He reacted to my disclosure with open sympathy.

"I just don't know what to do. We have to think first of the company that you have worked so hard to establish."

"Certainly. Branden-Moore is our priority."

"You know what a vast amount of material I read. I simply must be able to rely totally on a qualified assistant."

Mr. Moore leaned forward, soft, veined hands folded together in front of him. "What if I talked to her?"

"It will do no good. I have discussed this with her time and again."

"Then there is nothing else we can do," he stated decisively." You must find another assistant." After a long hesitation, he spoke again, "Remember that young fellow I introduced you to at our last party? I found him very impressive. Why not give him a try? I often run across him at the golf course."

"But what about April?" I asked with a moan. "I don't feel as if I...I don't have the heart..."

"You just leave everything to me, Cathy." As always, he was inclined to be generous. "April has been with the company for a long time. I will offer her an option, perhaps as manager of the secretarial pool."

"Thank you, Mr. Moore. You have been like a father to me all these years. What would I ever do without you?"

He smiled gravely. "Tell April I want to see her."

How did April know I myself had talked to Luther Moore? She flatly refused the secretarial offer and refused to speak a word to me after moving her belongings from my office.

I felt heartsick over this totally despicable act, over the fact that I had allowed Winston to manipulate me.

And I paid dearly, for April's absence left a great void. She had been the one friend of my youth whose affection had stayed throughout the many changes the years had brought. I missed her jokes, her laughter, and, most of all, her efficiency. With Winston as my assistant, my own workload doubled. I found I could not depend on his judgment, as I had on April's. And that meant bringing more and more work home to review myself.

But at times, when Winston smiled, brought me

coffee, kissed me--I felt that keeping Winston in my life had been the only alternative I had been given.

Of course, I was wrong and was soon forced to acknowledge it.

"What happened to that book that was on my desk? *New York Night?*"

"I recommended it and passed it on to the board for final approval."

"Books submitted to the board must go through me and Mr. Moore."

Winston flashed an appealing smile, one usually able to turn opposition into support. "Doesn't that slow down the process?"

"That *is* the process." Because I had planned to reject the book, I seethed with anger over how he had deliberately gone over my head.

For a while, months even, my days, though not smooth, were at least tolerable. I had always looked forward to the mid-morning break, to the long-established habit of taking coffee for myself and a special blend of tea for Luther Moore, into his office--more as a reminder for Mr. Moore to take his pills than for refreshment. I found that lately I needed more than ever this time of serenity, the steadiness an old friendship, to balance against the turmoil caused by Winston's intrusion into my office.

One Monday morning I set the tray on my desk

and left to search for some notes I had jotted down concerning a book under consideration. When I returned, I caught Winston sprinkling a substance of white powder from a small, brown bottle into Luther Moore's tea.

Startled, I drew to a halt. Waves of horror, of realization, swept over me. "What are you doing?" I demanded.

Winston, large, dark eyes rising to mine, slipped the bottle deep into his jacket pocket before he said. "What I'm doing will in no way harm him."

Still aghast, as if he had not answered at all, I spoke louder, "What did you stir into his tea?"

Winston shook his head as if it were of no consequence. "It will only make him…just a little sick."

"Why?" I gasped. "Why on earth would you want him ill?"

"Don't go on so." Winston's manner, the shrug of broad shoulders, the flash of white teeth, was disarming. "You would think I was planning to murder him."

"Exactly what are you planning?"

"Only for him to see for himself…that it is time for him to retire."

"But he doesn't want…"

"Cathy, darling! I am doing this for you! Moore could linger on as president way past your prime, and I want more than anything else to see you in charge of Branden-Moore!"

"I will have no part of this," I said, but I found that I could not move away from him, or drop my gaze from the dark depths of his large eyes.

"You deserve this break, Cathy, while you are still filled with vigor and ideas! I only want to see you get your chance; he's had his. And it can be done without actually putting him in any danger. Call it a little push into retirement. This drink," he said looking deep into the liquid again, "is a prod, reminding him that he is already old and sick. When he decides for himself to retire, you will find that we've done him a great favor. He will have the time he deserves to rest, to enjoy. Just trust me, Cathy. Do as I say, and I will make all your dreams happen for you!"

I could not actually believe that my own hands carried that tray into Luther Moore's office and placed it, as I was accustomed to do, between us on his huge, polished desk. When he saw me, he smiled and like an obedient child began spreading pills out on a napkin-- huge yellow ones, blue ones, tiny, white capsules. My heart plummeted. What effect might this foreign drug have on the others? What if I should be the instrument of killing Luther Moore, my best, perhaps my only, real friend?

After a careful sorting of medicine, he looked up

and asked, "Have you read the manuscript I gave you Friday? *Blind Faith*."

"That novel, just like the one the board is pressuring us to publish, *New York Night*, is not for us," I answered quickly. "Although one of the big, commercial houses will be glad to snap it up. It is crass, full of alarming and vulgar scenes that have no point. Without doubt," I added scornfully, "it will be a real money-maker."

"We always agree," he said with great satisfaction. His blue eyes held mine. They were such a pure color, wholly unpolluted. I felt a quaking start in my limbs, and I groped for the chair behind me and sank into it.

"A book, like a person, must be moral, must be accountable. This book, however action-packed, however on the surface, alluring, has an undercurrent of the deadliest corruption. It fails to come up to the standard our readers have come to expect from Branden-Moore."

Mr. Moore selected a pill and reached for the teacup. Quickly, I rose and snatched up the tray. "I forgot to put this in the microwave," I said and hurriedly exited his office. I carried it back into my office and slammed it down in front of Winston, who was lounging in my desk-chair. He scarcely looked up from the book my boss and I had just been discussing, *Blind Faith*.

No Longer Drifting
Jackson-Britton

I had stood silently by as Winston Kincade had taken over my home, my office, but this horror I could not allow. "There is a limit!" I said fervently. "You are to leave Luther Moore completely alone! If you don't, I will take some action to see to it that you do!"

"You're only working against yourself," he said matter-of-factly. "But you don't fool me. I know just how desperately you want his job. I was only helping you get what you desire most. But I can't force the decision; it's yours, if you make that choice."

I had finally drawn the line, but that wasn't the end of it. I had not a scrap of evidence, yet in the recesses of my mind I was certain that Winston Kincade's strange mixture still found its way into Mr. Moore's office. Every passing week my friend and boss appeared to grow paler, more profoundly weak, until at last he seemed to weave and stumble when he walked and those nearby felt it necessary to offer a steadying hand.

The board members began to inquire about the state of his health and to wonder if he should not think of retirement.

I agonized during long, sleepless nights. After having brought about the downfall of April Stenson, who was a valuable employee, would I ever be able to get Winston Kincade fired, too? He had become very popular with the staff, even with Mr. Moore himself. How could I face my boss with this incredible story and expect him to believe me and act on it?

Because I had the highest regard for Luther Moore, I knew I must take a stand against Winston whatever the risk. I would go to Luther Moore and tell him all, plead with him to fire Winston Kincade and drive him out of my office, out of my life! But I remained silent too long.

The following Tuesday Luther Moore collapsed and was rushed to Houston Memorial. I followed after the ambulance in my car and stayed for many tense, fearful hours in the waiting room until the doctor told me I could see him.

Mr. Moore sat, propped against pillows, which looked as white as his skin. I fought against tears, and sinking down beside his bed, I grasped his hand. "What is wrong with you? Did the doctors tell you anything?"

"I haven't wanted to worry you, Cathy," he said, "but for a long time I have been feeling increasingly sick and dizzy, unable to concentrate. Dr. Wiseman tells me it is stress that works against my heart condition." He smiled bravely. "But I tell him it is old age. Cathy, my dear, it must be faced. I have put off retirement years longer than the hardiest of my peers. It is time I step down." He paused. "How grateful I am to have you to carry on for me...to bless you, who I have so carefully chosen."

I shrank from the earnestness of his blue eyes.

But, also, I breathed easier. Luther Moore had survived, was safe, and I was now the president of Branden-Moore.

Even though I lacked the evidence to connect Winston with what had happened to Mr. Moore, my relationship with him had never the less suffered an irreparable blow.

"Don't keep blaming me! You're more guilty than I am," he accused. "Moore was never a friend of mine! It was you who betrayed him!"

In the face of our constant bickering, our outright shouting, Winston soon stormed, with clothes, dog, and computer, from my home and leased a small apartment closer to the company.

All alone, I faced another jolting fact: where the board had been afraid to cross Luther Moore, they had no such fear of me.

I had not fully realized the immensity of my new role, the difficulty, the impossibility, of trying to replace a man of such immeasurable scope and profundity.

The board began making demands: publish *Blind Faith*, which had, like *New York Night,* without my knowledge, been turned over directly to them; reorganize the printing department; alter the company's guidelines. Without Luther Moore and April Stenson, I had not one loyal supporter. I tried to be strong, to hold my line, but every day found me taking my stand a little further back, holding on to less and less ground.

Winston, now vice-president in charge of my old office, emerged as a constant threat. However much he smiled and appeared to cooperate, I knew he never gave a single thought to me or to the good of Branden-Moore. I noted how successfully he began setting himself up as indispensable, with what skill he undermined me to the board, so that all goals and concerns were presented first to him. I saw, resented, but I could not begin to match his slyness, his native capacity for manipulation.

Winston's sole concern was self. He roamed the halls like a predator, always in the shadows, biding his time, waiting for my final weakening which would summon an attack.

To make matters worse, Luther Moore, when I visited him, seemed to have lost all heart, to become singularly apathetic.

The situation worsened month after month. I should not have been surprised when at close of the fiscal year, at January's major board meeting, citing decreasing profits, increasing dissension, the board asked for my resignation as the company's president.

I could only stare down the long, shiny table past the rows of expensively dressed men and women, toward Winston Kincade. He gazed back at me, his eyes, dark and luminous.

Must I release the reign of my presidency to such a man?

Without comment, I rose. Heads turned and watched me as I forced myself to take one measured step then another across the great, carpeted hall.

Once in the lobby, I ducked into the restroom and splashed my face with cold water. I was still shaking when, sometime later, I returned to the office I had occupied since Luther Moore's resignation.

Inside, Winston Kincade was seated behind my desk. Mr. Moore's great swivel chair creaked as he swung toward me, saying almost jovially, "That picture of Fred Branden is going to have to go."

Stiffening, I crossed to the closet and as calmly as I could removed my coat and purse from the rack.

Winston spoke again just as I reached the door. "Cathy."

I turned around, appalled by his too-bright eyes, his gleaming, half-smile. "You don't have to leave," he said ever so casually. "You can stay and work for me."

Without answering, I turned my back on him and hurried out into the busy street. Not knowing where I was going, almost in a panic, I got into my car and zigzagged in and out of traffic, only half-aware through the blur of tears, of the changing lights, of the cars careening in and out of lanes. I ended up at Luther Moore's serene, rock house on the outskirts of the city.

He sat huddled in front of a dying fire, a flannel robe draped across his thin shoulders. He looked so very frail, so very old. Before I could speak to him, he said, "I know."

"You've got to help me!" I cried. "We are losing total control of the company!"

Luther Moore smiled wanly and told me, "The moment I stepped down, the board became the power. They are not like me."

"Isn't there anything you can do?"

He gave a feeble shake of his head. "I have tried time and again to intervene in your behalf. But, Cathy, they don't listen to me anymore."

"Don't they realize how much they owe you?" I demanded incredulously. "You are a founder of this company!"

"But no longer the major investor," he reminded me.

"Surely you can sway them. You're the one who made Branden-Moore what it is!"

"Times change very quickly," he said. "Often in an adverse way. But only those directly involved in the activity have the power to stop it." He stared toward the last lapping of the flames around the burned-out wood. "The lessons it took me a lifetime to learn, they find irrelevant. They are hell-bent on tearing down, on undoing all the work, all the accomplishments of those many, difficult..." His hollow voice drifted off and blended into the solemn quietness.

I drew in my breath. "You counted on me to bear the standard for you!" Tears welled in my eyes.

Luther Moore watched me, the old admiration and affection returning to his finely chiseled features. "What I have always seen in you, Cathy, is an ability to quickly discern right from wrong—along with the strength to stand up for your beliefs."

He continued, so certain of me. "Even when you make mistakes, and we all do, you accept blame. How necessary that is. It is the only brake to a downhill course."

The fire in the grate flared again, then ceased burning. As it extinguished, the illusion of light and warmth vanished and I felt gripped by a consuming chill.

I myself had brought Winston Kincade into power. My silence, my lack of opposition, had confined Branden-Moore to ruin.

Luther Moore said soothingly, "Because you possess those very special traits, everything, in the end, is going turn all right for you."

In another venture, perhaps. But Branden-Moore was no longer ours. Winston Kincade had fed the unthinking board with flattery, with lies, with promises—he had taken over! And I had allowed him to do it! I could not control my tears. My anguished sobs echoed in the still room.

Luther Moore leaned forward, and his frail hand in an expression of deep consolation, patted mine. "Remember this, my dear," he said, "You are not to blame."

On a Padre Island pier, a brother and sister share a special moment of closeness that defies even death.

THE SEA GOD

"Do you have to tag along everywhere I go?" Jim turned to ask in annoyance. This did nothing to slow my dogged steps as I trudged down the pier after him. He reached back and snatched the hat from my head and held it high above my reach.

"Give that back!" I cried, making a lunge for it. My brother was fourteen years old that summer, three years older and six inches taller than me.

He tossed the hat back on my head with an undignified plop. "It's a stupid hat," he said as I carefully adjusted its brim over my pigtails. "And you look stupid in it."

"It's my hat and it's on my head and I like it!" I didn't really know why I had taken to wearing Jim's old, castoff canvas hat with the floppy brim all the time. I had simply put it on one afternoon at the beginning of summer and since then had rarely taken it off. It seemed to have become a part of me, and now I felt as strange and naked without it as I would feel without my T-shirt and shorts or even my underwear.

Jim stalked on along the fishing pier and I followed at a safe distance. The argument didn't faze me. We fought all the time. In fact we had quarreled all the way to Padre Island. Mom swore she could hear our loud voices from the back of the camper clear up to the front pickup seat, and Dad had threatened more than once to turn around and go back home before we ever got to the ocean.

But now we were here and I could smell the salt spray and hear the crash of the waves. It was not a sight you would ever see back home in Kansas. We passed a few fishermen as we walked the length of the pier, then we were alone on the very end. The sight of the vast, endless ocean seemed to get to Jim too, because when we reached the end of the pier he relented and let me sit down beside him without a fuss. Despite our many disagreements, we could sometimes be as close as two people could be, sometimes we completed each other's sentences and thoughts.

"It's the prettiest sight I've ever seen," I sighed.

Jim didn't answer, just continued to stare out to sea as if he had never seen anything like it before, either, as if the ebb and lull of the tide entranced him. The crowning of the waves as they beat with such force against the wooden legs of the pier made the ocean a little scary, too. I shivered, in awe of its violence, its loneliness, its absolute power.

"Do you think there's sea monsters out there?"

"Don't be dumb!" His scorn quickly silenced me. He continued to gaze in awe at the ceaseless waves. "It's the Sea God who's out there."

I swallowed hard. The methodical rise and fall of the waves made the sea appear a living, breathing thing. You could almost believe that there was such a being in the midst of all that pounding fury. I could almost see his transparent form, a bronze-green, bearded Poseidon, arms uplifted, rising from the waves. I knew the image came from a picture Jim had shown me from a library book, of an old Greek statue that had been pulled up from a shipwreck on the ocean floor.

Jim took on the moody look he had been adopting lately. "We should make a sacrifice."

"What should we give him?" My voice quavered a little. Jim had also been reading books about the Aztecs lately, and in the back of my mind I feared he might mean human sacrifice, namely, a bothersome kid sister.

"Only our most prized possessions are worthy," he replied, then added seriously, "Just trust me. What you treasure will be safe out there."

He thought for a moment, then drew the silver skull ring from his finger. As far as I knew, the heavy silver ring, the envy of his classmates, left his hand less often than my hat left my head.

I drew in a gasp of admiration as, without a moment's hesitation, as if it were nothing to him, he tossed the heavy piece of silver into the boiling foam, where it quickly vanished, as if it had been consumed by a vengeful god.

Jim turned to look at me. "Now the hat."

I clutched the brim of my hat possessively, stubbornly. "No! I don't want to!"

"If you keep it, you'll grow tired of it and it'll just be another old hat to you. If you give it up now," Jim said, stroking the pale spot on his finger where the ring had been, "It will become immortal."

Such romantic notions often appealed to him. Jim had, in one of his brooding moods, read to me from his favorite book of poems one by Browning called *Prophyria's Lover,* about a man who strangled his love with her own, long hair to make her his forever.

No Longer Drifting
Jackson-Britton

But no amount of idealism could convince me to sacrifice my precious hat.

"It's mine! It's mine!" I began running back down the pier, away from Jim, away from the evil creature behind him who now demanded a token of me, a piece of my soul.

"Selfish, that's what you are!" Jim called after me, and his form seemed suddenly inhumanly tall, his voice, the thunder of Poseidon. "Too selfish to give to the Sea God his dues. You've cursed us. From now on, only bad things will happen to us."

Jim was right—on two counts. By the end of the summer I had grown tired of the hat. It had become just another object to me, another possession. I began to wear my hair long, and loose, like Prophyria, its straight, sun-bleached locks reaching the small of my back. I wore the hat less and less often until at the end of the season it lay abandoned in a trunk in the back of the closet with my other cast-off summer things. The guilt stayed with me. At the least, I felt regretful, as if I had spoiled something beautiful by trying to hang on to it. At the most, I felt as if I had done something terribly wrong, as if I had secretly evoked the wrath of some vengeful deity.

The next summer, Jim went back to Padre Island with his friends over school vacation. They rented a small fishing boat. Far out to sea, the boat capsized and though the other two boys were saved, my brother was washed overboard, leaving my parents crushed and empty hulls, leaving me adrift at sea.

As years passed we gradually claimed the pieces of our broken lives. I finished college, left home, found a job in Europe with a tour company. I never returned to the ocean again. I could not get into a boat, and even flying over in a plane, as my work often required, left me anxious and queasy.

* * *

"Lady, are you all right?" Gentle hands shook me uncertainly. I woke with a start, realizing that I was on the plane, heading home.

"I'm fine," I replied, giving a shaky smile to my seatmate, hoping I hadn't cried out aloud. I turned back to the window and pressed my face against the glass. We were crossing the Atlantic. Below us, I could see only water, and I felt my mouth go dry. Even from this height, the same dream, the nightmare, seemed to extend itself into life. Near-invisible, grasping hands reached up to me from the depths of the sea. I closed my eyes but dared not sleep.

At the airport I rented a car. I rolled down the window, letting in the heat and smell of Kansas summer, of fields of corn and wheat and dry land. As I turned into the driveway, I saw how broken-down the old house had become. I sent money home regularly, but Mom and Dad spent it on other things, on necessities, on groceries and prescriptions.

Dad met me at the door. It had been several years since I had last seen him, and the long absence gave the illusion that he had grown old overnight, like the picture of Dorian Gray.

"How is Mom?" I whispered.

"About the same." Dad shook his head. "Always the same..." "Mom huddled on the old recliner near the fireplace, even though the room was not cold. The sight of her, just as at Jim's funeral, shattered my heart. She had never recovered from losing Jim, had managed only to live on without will or spirit.

"I should never have let him take that trip." She looked at me with despairing eyes, but saw only Jim. "He would have listened to me, Laura."

I took her hand and felt it's winter chill. I wanted to say, "Mom, why can't you just let him go?" But who was I to ask her that? I hadn't gotten over Jim's death, either; I had just run away, off to Europe, half-afraid to ever return home.

The night before I left, I found the hat in a trunk in the attic, battered and wrinkled, but no worse for the passage of time. I pressed it to my cheek, closed my eyes, and thought of Jim.

It was as if I could see, through his eyes, those last desperate moments when the boat had capsized and he had been pulled under by the waves. Like Mom, I was tormented by all of the ways I had failed him. It was me, not her, he would have listened to. Why hadn't I begged him not to go?

Suddenly, I felt a surrounded by a strange sense of peace. It was almost as if Jim were in the room with me, as if I heard his voice saying, as it had on the pier that day, "Just trust me. What you treasure most will be safe out there."

After I left my folks' house, I didn't go back to the airport. Instead, I turned the rental car south and drove. I wasn't aware of day or night, only road maps and my mission.

Dusk was falling when I reached the pier on Padre Island. Time seemed to fall back, until I could imagine I was a child again, and that Jim was there, beside me. The wind and salt spray whipped at my face. I hurled the hat high into the air. I watched it for a long time, a white spot, bobbing like the head of some drowning man upon the waves before it disappeared forever into the waiting sea.

No Longer Drifting
Jackson-Britton

Lattimer was losing something important in his life—the old man's complete confidence. How far was he willing to go to keep it?

THE BIG EXCEPTION

Lattimer, accustomed to respect and compliance from others in his office, felt a surge of anger at his boss for again giving Clark's opinion more credence than his. He wanted to be petulant, but left the room without showing his frustration. Afterwards, the force of his feelings, surfacing more and more often in everything he did, disturbed him: it seemed the manifestation of deep, ugly egotism, and Lattimer recognized it as he would have recognized the growing evidence of disease.

No Longer Drifting
Jackson-Britton

His wife met him at the door with a kiss. "You look as if you've had a tough day."

"It's a tough world," he replied—no smile, just sank into his chair. "I think I'll just sit here awhile."

"Want the T.V.?"

"No"

Barbara switched it off on her way to the kitchen.

Lattimer pushed the recliner back and stared at his carefully polished shoes. The basic issue--did he think it necessary for the company to fire Melvin Willer—didn't seem to Lattimer to be the issue at all. He found himself resenting everything Clark had said today. He particularly resented the fact that Patterson, the boss, had been so attentive to Clark. Lattimer had never feared Clark as a competitor; he was just distraught because Clark, in his forceless way, had won Patterson over again, while Lattimer's pitch had proven powerless.

Lattimer's apprehension increased. Clark was too easy, too inclined to be generous; but now Lattimer began to wonder if Patterson and Clark were right. Perhaps it was possible to overlook the lost account and salvage Melvin Willer. Melvin Willer, the man, whether he went or stayed, meant nothing to Lattimer. Suddenly he felt very weary. Maybe he should drop the matter and let Clark have this one. Lattimer had more important things to do.

No Longer Drifting
Jackson-Britton

Even as Lattimer thought this, his arguments to regain stature began to form in his mind. The master salesman took over. He knew that in the end he would convince Patterson, just as he had done for so many years. But this time, for some reason, he experienced doubts.

Lattimer kept going over what they had said at the meeting. Patterson's tone, or maybe his face, suggested that Lattimer was losing something very important in his life—the old man's complete confidence.

"I wish you wouldn't bring your work home with you," Barbara said.

Despite Barbara's protests, his projection of what he was going to say and do first thing tomorrow lasted the entire evening, and feeling ill at ease and impatient in the huge outer office the next day, Lattimer went over it for a final rehearsal.

Willer sat at his desk, studying papers, as if he were deeply perplexed and shaken, or embarrassed that his blunder was the talk of the company. The light from the window made his hair and face look gray.

The office began filling with the clatter of early arrivers. Lattimer returned their small talk and banter. Neither the salesmen nor Lattimer looked at Willer. It was as if Melvin Willer had already cleaned out his desk and left.

No Longer Drifting
Jackson-Britton

Clark entered. The big, slow-moving man made his way through rows of desks, pausing to speak and listen to one and another along his path. He stopped in front of Willer's desk. "Let's get some coffee, Melvin."

"No. No, thanks." The grayness had attached itself to Willer's voice. "I was going to look over Golden's records again."

Regardless of what he does now, Lattimer thought, Willer knows he can't win Golden back. It was appealing or pathetic—Lattimer didn't know which—to see Willer still struggling to amend something so overwhelmingly hopeless.

"The only thing you can do," Clark said in a kindly way, "is make a counter-proposal. Let Golden have his way. Golden's temperamental, give him all the toys now, he'll be willing to share later."

"It doesn't sound fair," Willer replied, frowning, "not to deal the same with everyone."

"You were very skillful in handling Bud Marks last week. Use some of those tactics with Golden."

Lattimer felt irritated that Clark was so willing to waste his time, but time didn't mean much to Clark as it did to Lattimer. He did not hear what Willer answered as he saw his boss gesturing to him from the glass-paneled doorway.

"Jim, if I recall," Patterson said as Lattimer entered his office, "it was you who landed Tommy Golden's account. I think you should be the one to 'gather him back into the fold,' so to speak."

"The impossible you hand over to me." Lattimer sat down in the chair he usually chose. "Much thanks."

Patterson smiled a playful, youthful smile that no longer matched the frail form or the startlingly white hair. "We need him," he said, and smiled again.

Patterson was an immensely busy man who appreciated the fact that Lattimer waylaid most of the problems before they reached him; so the smile was often present when he talked to Lattimer. But this time the look of affection and approval was mixed with anxiousness. He's afraid he's offended me, Lattimer thought; he's willing to make concessions.

Lattimer slowly removed a cigarette from the case and lit it. Purposely he smoked and said nothing. Patterson watched him, his quick mind busy with questions, but too much the pro to ask them. So each waited, until finally Lattimer determined the waiting had been to his advantage. He squashed out the cigarette. "I think we made the wrong decision about Willer," he said. The *we* took the offensiveness out of *wrong*.

"I don't admit this to everyone," Patterson said, "but every once in a while I have a human feeling." He smiled again. "Willer has three kids and no wife."

"He acquired those problems, too," Lattimer observed. "We didn't."

"Willer might work out in time. Clark seems to think we haven't given him much assistance."

Lattimer's answer was his direct gaze.

Patterson leaned back in the swivel chair. The look of doubt caused his alert eyes to narrow. "Willer really needs this job," Patterson said.

"Needs the job and can do the job are two different concepts. We've probably lost Tommy Golden's account for good." Lattimer's voice lowered. "You might not care, but I've invested time in it. Years."

Patterson straightened up in his chair and said brightly, "I believe you can talk Golden back."

"I'll talk to Golden, but I don't think it's going to do any good. That's not going to remedy the problem. The problem is Melvin Willer. His blunders are much too expensive."

As he always did before committing himself, Patterson rose from his chair to stand by the large bay window. Lattimer listened to the sounds of the early morning traffic as he waited.

"It makes a difference to you, that much difference, does it, Jim?"

"Not to me, to the company. Willer's too big a risk."

"After our meeting last night, Clark believes we're going to keep him."

"Clark won't hold you to it. He hardly knows Willer."

Patterson turned around and leaned against the window ledge. With a sense of relief, Lattimer could feel the return of Patterson's total trust, the handing back of control, the power he had lost. "Will you let me replace him?" he asked his boss.

"Go ahead."

* * *

Lattimer strode through the outer office where Clark was negotiating with two men from Baxter's. At a glance Lattimer could tell each of them opposed the other's opinion. Clark, trying to convince them of something, was patient and affable—a manner not likely to carry much weight with these two. The bearded man looked disenchanted; the elderly man, stubborn. Let Clark handle this himself, Lattimer thought, as he swerved around them. He had other things to do.

He sat down at his desk, pressed a button and said, "Janet, send Melvin Willer in."

Several minutes later Janet's voice announced. "Mr. Willer is out of the office. I'll tell him you want to see him the minute he comes in."

No Longer Drifting
Jackson-Britton

"All right." Lattimer wanted to get it over with and it showed in his abrupt "Thank you."

Clark and the two men from Baxter's ended up in Lattimer's office. With skillful strategy employed for over an hour, Lattimer persuaded them to accept a position little different from Clark's original offer.

After the handshakes and their leaving, Clark lingered. "Well you've done it again!" he said heartily.

"Done what?"

"Won them to our side. Made them change their minds. I didn't think it could be done." Clark grinned. "It's a hell of a gift," he said, then added, "When you're right, that is."

Lattimer looked at him sharply. He wasn't at all used to Clark's being critical of him. Clark's admiration and support was something dependable, something he had perhaps unconsciously grown to expect. He frowned. "I didn't think I gave them too much."

Clark chuckled. "No, Jim, you never do that. I'm referring to Melvin Willer."

"You're still on that."

"I've talked to Mr. Patterson this morning," Clark said. "You're not right about Willer, Jim. He's smart. He could be valuable to us."

Lattimer said nothing.

"Golden likes a talker, a dealer. He detests Willer's conservatism. But some people would consider

Willer's strong point, a man like Jeff Page, for instance. We just didn't take the time…"

"I never took him to raise," Lattimer answered.

"Losing this job is really going to hurt him. That doesn't matter to you?"

"When you're through with that file, will you leave it with Janet?"

Clark picked up on the dismissal, but at the door, stopped again. His usually calm face appeared troubled. "You've got a lot going for you, Jim," he said quietly; then he added, "with one big exception."

* * *

Clark's words and manner rankled him. Clark wasn't going to succeed, he told himself, in making him feel guilty. Lattimer took out Tommy Golden's file, but it was difficult for his excited mind to form substantial stepping-stones that would reach Golden— if Golden could be reached.

On the phone Golden sounded irreversibly angry; but that didn't mean he couldn't change his mind, did it? Lattimer knew Golden liked him; that's why they had won the account in the first place. His agreeing to meet Lattimer at the club was a good sign.

Janet's voice interrupted his thoughts. "Mr. Willer is here now, Mr. Lattimer."

"Send him in."

No Longer Drifting
Jackson-Britton

The tall, thin man approached the desk saying "no thank you" when Lattimer indicated a chair. He stood very straight. Direct light from the window intensified shades of gray, especially around the corners of his mouth.

Willer's pale eyes held Lattimer's gaze. It was the first time Lattimer had really looked at him. Somehow, he had expected anything but this--this intelligence, this determination to make the best of everything even in the face of certain defeat.

Because it was Lattimer's nature to think everything through, he was surprised at himself for having never considered the actual words he would use. We have decided to let you go—no. You're just not right for this particular company—no. While sentences formed and reformed in his mind, Willer, as if trying to make things easier for him, spoke, "I've already talked to Clark."

So Clark had prepared him.

"Everyone in the whole office knows," Willer continued. "I guess there's no need for us to talk about it."

For something to do, Lattimer opened the file on his desk and jogged papers through his fingers. Before he looked up again, an odd thing happened. It seemed as if he were Melvin Willer and Melvin Willer were he. He shook his head trying to dissolve the vision, but the vision persisted and in the face of it, Lattimer's apprehension mounted.

Clark had been right! Lattimer himself could have prevented the Golden disaster had he been willing to help Willer, had he given him any time or thought.

Lattimer knew he was experiencing a change of heart, seeing the situation in another light. But it was too late for that! It was too late now to do anything but fire him.

Willer was the talk of the office. Everyone knew Patterson had given him the go-ahead to terminate Willer today. Lattimer must fire Willer now to preserve his own executive image; after all, firing Melvin Willer was his idea, and what sort of man hasn't the fortitude to carry out his own decisions?

"Why I sent for you," Lattimer said brusquely, then he stopped short. "Why I sent for you…"He started again, gazing at the open file in his hand, "is because I want to trade accounts with you. I'll give you Jeff Page's account, you give me Tommy Golden's."

No Longer Drifting
Jackson-Britton

The father of a seriously ill newborn is forced to make a decision no parent should ever have to make

BABY UNDER GLASS

When Don first saw his son, he had to turn away, sickened by the sight of twisting tubes and pumping machinery. Faye's hysterical weeping was like a knife twisting again and again in his heart. "Don't Honey. Please, don't." He tried to put his arm around his wife, but she recoiled from him, as if his touch was painful, and covered her face with her hands.

"I'll take her back to her room," the nurse said. "You can stay a while longer, if you like."

"No!" Don wanted to scream out after them. "Don't leave me alone in here!"

He paced the short, glass-enclosed length of the intensive care unit, watching Faye and the nurse disappear down the hallway. The heavy-set nurse was bracing Faye, practically holding her up. He wondered if her feet were even touching the ground. His beautiful, flighty Faye. Her long, wavy hair was loose and disheveled above the shapeless hospital gown, making her look more than ever like some pale fairy-child. How was she ever going to handle this?

How was he going to handle it? Don turned back toward the incubator where, under still another layer of glass, their baby of forty-eight hours struggled for life, struggled against virtually impossible odds.

The Neo-Natal Unit put Don in mind of a space capsule. He himself felt n in the green gown and mask they made everyone wear when they entered. Their baby lay alone in a special, isolated place where he could be constantly monitored by what looked like a television screen.

Don peered through the glass at the jungle of tubes, liquids, and plastic. The baby lay motionless. The only sign of movement was the rise and fall of the mechanical respirator, forcing and expelling air from the tiny chest, keeping the small lungs breathing. Don slumped into the chair by the incubator, which he shared with a huge, grinning red bear.

When Don turned his head, he felt a sudden rush of dizziness.

No Longer Drifting
Jackson-Britton

The events of the past two days and nights came back to him in fragments. He recalled driving Faye to the hospital, how she had patted her bulging stomach, delighted over the early signs of labor. "I'm glad," she had told him. I want to get back to my dancing. I'm so sick of maternity clothes, I could just scream!"

Once more he heard Dr. Brentwood, the obstetrician, saying, "We'll know soon whether it's true labor or a false alarm."

By late afternoon, there was no doubt. Faye's sharp cries of pain seemed to fill up every empty space in the tense, antiseptic labor room.

Don closed his eyes tightly, but still the images persisted—shadowy white figures racing Faye out on a stretcher toward surgery. Dr. Moore telling him, "The baby is in distress. We're going to have to do an emergency Caesarian."

Don tried to follow the stretcher.

A nurse's hands, firm but gentle, prevented him from entering the operating room. "I'm sorry, but you'll have to wait outside."

Don remembered his stunned feeling as the door closed in his face. He had promised Faye he would be there for her. He remembered staring after the nurse, staring helplessly through those tiny glass windows of the operating room, straining to catch a last glimpse of Faye.

No Longer Drifting
Jackson-Britton

The past two days and nights had been a blur of worry, pacing, and medical jargon he didn't understand. He only knew that Faye was out of danger. But their baby was born seriously premature; their baby was in distress.

What a mockery the grinning bear, with its semblance of normality, seemed now. It was larger than the baby itself. Don thought about the things at home, the bassinet, the baseball pajamas. He was tired, his mouth tasted bitter from countless Styrofoam cups of coffee. He was ready to wake from this ugly dream. He longed to be back in his bed, sleeping, pregnant Faye nestled comfortably in his arms. He glanced down at his stiff, new teddy bear companion and wanted to cry.

Much later, Don left the Neo-Natal Unit and returned to Faye's room on the maternity ward. She was asleep. The sound of her heavy, even breathing told him that she had probably been sedated.

"Faye."

Faye stirred, then blinked. She looked frightened, as if she didn't know exactly where she was. Then her eyes focused upon Don. A ghost of a smile crossed her lips.

"How do you feel?" Don asked.

The smile crumpled. "I hurt, Don. I hurt all over."

No Longer Drifting
Jackson-Britton

Don held her, rocking her back and forth as if she was a small child. "I know, Honey. I know."

"It was such a shock, seeing our baby like that." She sobbed into his arms. "All those tubes and things!"

They moved apart as Dr. Cabral stepped into the room. The neonatal specialist was a young man, small-boned and very dark-skinned. Don thought he might be from India or Pakistan. His English was perfect, but his voice so soft that Don often had to lean close to understand his words.

"The baby is holding his own." With no smile on his face, no sign of hope or reassurance, Dr. Cabral added. "Time is such a critical factor. Now that he's passed through the first forty-eight hours, there's a fighting chance."

"Thank God," Don whispered.

Dr. Cabral glanced at Fay, then his dark eyes moved back to Don. "He's still a very sick baby." A moment of silence followed. The doctor hesitated as if carefully choosing his words. "A few years ago, an infant this small would not even have had a chance of survival."

"I'm so grateful something can be done."

A shadow crossed the doctor's face, reflected itself in his somber, dark eyes. "Modern science is sometimes a mixed blessing. We're taking all measures possible to save his life. The respirator will keep the baby breathing, but the increased oxygen levels may cause blindness or permanent brain damage."

"Brain damage…"The skin at the base of Don's neck prickled with an uncomfortable warmth, like the beginnings of a fever.

Whatever color was left drained from Faye's pale face. "You mean, even if he does pull through, our baby may not be…normal?"

"We'll try to wean him off the respirator as soon as possible. And hope for a miracle."

***

As soon as the doctor left, Don and Faye went to see the baby again. At this late hour, they did not attempt to don gowns or go into the cubicle where the incubator lay. They only peered helplessly at their baby through two layers of outside glass. The infant, so tiny he could fit into the palm of a hand, clung by such a tenuous thread to life.

"We should name him," Don said finally. If it was a boy, they had talked about calling him Daniel, after Don's father.

"Let's wait," Faye said, and turned her face away from him.

She was staring with morbid fascination at the baby, her eyes fastened on the tubes and IVs that surrounded him. Her mouth, white about the edges as if from some long illness, trembled. She could have been staring at a corpse in a casket instead of a newborn son.

Don found her hand and squeezed it. "He's going to make it, Faye. Our baby is going to be all right. We have to keep on believing that! We have to be strong."

She turned and looked up at him. Her eyes were shuttered now; they revealed nothing at all. How they frightened him, those hollow eyes.

* * *

Don took a shower every morning before work. It was his transition time, that hot, steamy limbo between a world of antiseptic silence and swift, jostling traffic. The smell of the hospital, would he ever get it out of his hair, his skin, his nostrils?

He dried off his hair, carefully avoiding his image in the mirror. The man with his deep-shadowed eyes was as much a stranger as the silent woman he left waiting in their home or at the hospital, a woman he barely recognized, who still called herself Faye, his wife.

Nearly a month had passed, and the baby—now officially named Daniel—still clung stubbornly to life. Don divided his time between work and the Neo-Natal Unit. He was glad for his job, the feeling of normality it gave him. His house, the bedroom, had become foreign to him, a never-world of blue sheets, flowered pictures, and remote-control television. It seemed in another life that he and Faye had tumbled, laughing, on those same blue designer sheets. Now Faye avoided their room, chose instead to sleep on the sofa, alone.

Don wondered if Faye secretly blamed him. It had been he, not Faye, who had wanted the baby in the first place. "I'm happy with the way things are—just the two of us. Why rush it?" she had insisted when he had first hinted about starting a family. Sometimes Don blamed himself for the nightmare he had put them through. They had been content; maybe this was his punishment for demanding more.

Don, showered and dressed, was alarmed to find Faye still in her bathrobe, her hair uncombed and tangled. She stood in the center of the bedroom, staring critically into the full-length mirror that hung on the closet door. "I'm fat," she said finally. "Look at me. I look all bloated and fat."

Faye, who prided herself on her trim, lean dancer's body, seemed appalled at the sight of her swollen breasts and soft, punchy stomach. Don came around behind her, putting his arms around her shoulders. "Honey, you just gave birth. It takes a little time to get back to normal."

Tears, unchecked, rolled down her cheeks. "Are things are never going to be normal again?"

He squeezed her shoulder slightly. "Darling, you have to get dressed. I'll be late for work." Every morning, Don dropped her off at the hospital so she could be with the baby. After supper, they both would come up and spend the evenings, sometimes all night with their son. It was as if their lives had been placed on some kind of an indefinite hold, a cycle without beginning or end.

"I'm not going."

"What do you mean?"

She shrugged. "The baby doesn't need me. The nurses take care of everything. So why do they need me there?"

"But don't you want to be with our baby?"

"He's not going to live! If he does live, what kind of a life will he have—what kind of a life will *we* have?" The hopelessness turned suddenly to anger, and she lashed out at him. "You still have your job! I have nothing! I can't take another day of sitting there, staring at that incubator, watching a baby that never cries, that hardly even moves. You don't know what it's like! Sometimes I think I'm going crazy. It's like someone has stolen my whole life away from me. I--I wish he'd never been born!"

"Oh, Faye—"

"Maybe this is God's way of punishing me for not wanting him in the first place!"

"Faye, I wish you wouldn't talk like this." The hysterical edge to her voice frightened Don. He put his arm around her shoulders. "You need a rest. I'll miss work and go to the hospital this afternoon. I'm going to call your mother and see if she can come over."

Faye hesitated, then brightened a little. "Okay." She was so much like a child herself, Don thought, her joy so easily shaken, her unhappiness so quickly pacified.

A half hour later, Don sat in Dr. Cabral's office, shaking a packet of cream into lukewarm coffee.

"I have good news for you," the doctor said, white teeth flashing against his dark skin. "The baby is showing a slight improvement. We may be able to try and wean him off the respirator in a few weeks." He smiled at Don. "Where's your wife this morning? Not ill, I hope. Premature infants need that personal contact with their mothers."

"This has been a real strain on her. I'm almost as worried about her as I am about the baby," Don confided. "She's been so depressed."

"The 'baby blues' are a fairly common, even when there are no complications," the doctor replied.

"It seems to go much deeper than that."

Dr. Cabral frowned a little, then took out a pad and wrote down a name. "If it lasts much longer, have her call this man."

Don looked up at him with a sense of dread. "A psychiatrist?"

No Longer Drifting
Jackson-Britton

"There's no need to be ashamed. She's going through a very traumatic time. She may need someone to talk to."

Why can't it be me? Don wondered as he took the paper and stuffed it into his shirt pocket. Why can't she talk to me?

Don stopped by once more to see the baby before leaving.

He found a strange sense of comfort being there with his son. Don peered through the glass, studying the tiny thatch of hair, the blunt features that had not yet taken on any character of their own. He thought he could see just a hint of himself about the nose, a little of Faye in the tiny, puckered mouth.

When Don came home, he found Faye in the bedroom, unpacking shopping bags. "How's the baby?" she asked. She never called him by his name.

"I've got some good news. The doctor says he's improving a little."

"Wonderful," she responded, but her voice sounded preoccupied and far away.

"Where did you go today?"

"Shopping. Oh, it was so good to get out again!" Faye pulled a pair of shimming black tights from the sack, then a black-and-white striped leotard. "After Mom went home, I stopped by the dance studio and talked to Aaron about going back to work soon. I—haven't had a chance to put supper on yet."

"That's okay. I thought we'd go out tonight. Just the two of us. Dinner and dancing."

"Could we?"

Don couldn't stop looking at her. Faye's long, brown hair fell in shining, freshly-washed waves about her face. She seemed in good spirits, even humming a little under her breath as she put away the leotards. For a moment, she was the old Faye again, the Faye who had been lost.

* * *

"I've been trying to reach you all evening." Dr. Cabral, a grave expression on his face, stepped toward them as they entered the Neo-Natal Unit.

Don felt his chest tighten, his muscles responding to the tension in the air. "What's wrong?"

"The baby has suffered a small hemorrhage." A deep frown creased the doctor's face. "Daniel's need for oxygen is beginning to exceed the level that is safe for his eyes and brain."

"What does that mean?"

"We suspect there may be some permanent eye or brain damage... we're still performing tests... we just don't know. I won't lead you on... things don't look good."

"But we had talked about weaning him off the respirator."

Dr. Cabral gravely shook his head. "No chance of that now. We are fighting just to keep him alive."

Don heard Faye and the doctor speaking in low voices, but he did not listen to their words. He was thinking about how hopeful the two of them had been just a few hours ago. The burden of dread and fear felt all the heavier for the brief respite. And now, just when things were starting to look up, he saw his world tottering again, on the verge of collapse.

***

As the days passed, the baby's condition grew more critical. Twice, on Saturday, Don left his watch by the incubator to visit the pay phone down the hall. The telephone rang into an empty room.

A vision of Faye crossed his mind, dressed in her leotards. A monotone voice on the stereo, an exercise instructor, had made the background for their angry words this morning.

"You don't care about the baby at all," he had accused when she had refused to go to the hospital with him. "I'm so damned sick of your selfishness!"

"What do you want me to do?" Faye had demanded in a voice that had gone shrill and defensive. "Sit by that incubator day and night until I'm a wasted out shell? Give up my whole life for him? I can't! I have to go on living, and you do, too!" Tears trembled in her voice. "He's not getting any better, Don. It's cruel for him to go on suffering when he doesn't even have a chance!" Even though Don expected her next words, they still felt painful to his ears. "He was never meant to be born. Sometimes, I wish he'd just--just--"

"Die?" Don demanded, his voice low and cruel. "Well, maybe you'll get your wish."

"That's not what I meant! I don't know! I just don't know anymore!"

Don had whirled away, toward the door.

"Where are you going, Don?" Faye's voice wavered.

"Back to the hospital. "

He had not asked her to come with him. Now, the bitter words rang in his mind, words that could never be taken back. He knew that Faye was gone. Even if she had not yet emptied her clothes from the drawers and closets, she had left him. To her, the baby was already dead.

* * *

Days merged into nights, one long, endless vigil. Don walked wearily down corridor to the pay phone by the window. Once more, he tried to call Faye, but the line was busy. He remembered the way she had looked the night she had left him. A stoniness had crept over her delicate features, making them seem hard, as if they

No Longer Drifting
Jackson-Britton

were carved of marble. Since Faye had moved out, Don no longer went home much to the empty house.

Dr. Cabral encountered Don outside of ICU and somberly drew him into his office. After a long silence, with a defeated sigh, he said, "Keeping Daniel alive now is going to take drastic measures. Our only hope involves a very risky surgery."

"Then we must take that chance."

Again, the silence. "I'm afraid it's not that simple. It is our hospital policy to look at each case individually, to weigh the risks with the projected outcome. I must caution you that even if he survives the surgery, the possibility is great that your son will suffer multiple handicaps."

"I want to do everything we can to save him!"

Dr. Cabral glanced away. "I've spoken to your wife. She has made her feelings known to me. You must be aware Faye is opposed to making any aggressive attempts to prolong Daniel's life."

Don felt a dull sense of shock. "Does that mean…"

"Although she has refused to sign the necessary forms to authorize the surgery, she will not prevent you from doing so if that is your wish."

"What—what are you saying?"

The doctor considered him with dark, troubled eyes. "The decision has been left up to you."

* * *

No Longer Drifting
Jackson-Britton

Don stepped into the isolated unit just as the nurse slipped out. He was alone with the incubator and giant red teddy bear, staring down at the baby under glass.

How he wished he could hold his son! He had the sudden urge to rescue him, to just push through that jungle of plastic and machinery and take him away. He longed to cradle him in his arms, feel his soft heartbeat against his chest.

What was right? To keep Daniel alive as long as he could, doomed to a life of dependency, or to refuse surgery and set him free? The decision was like a lead weight upon Don's shoulders. Such an awesome decision. Was he God, that he should have to make it?

Don thought fleetingly of the mounting hospital bills, his ruined marriage. If Daniel lived...the responsibility of raising a child with multiple handicaps alone frightened him. "Why?" Don found himself asking aloud. "Why did you ever have to be born?"

The baby stirred weakly. Instinctively, it made small sucking noises, tried to raise one of its frail, restrained fists to its mouth. For a moment, the weak, gray-black eyes opened, seemed to focus upon Don. They were cloudy and opaque, like the eyes of a newborn kitten. The tiny arms raised as if reaching for Don.

Don leaned closer and pressed his fingers to the glass. He could feel a bond of love penetrate the invisible wall between them. No matter what the outcome, he knew at that moment that he would fight for his child, fight to the bitter end.

"My son," he whispered. He wondered if Daniel really did see him. Did the baby know he could not give him up?

Because Harold hadn't known or cared what Ellen thought or how she felt, he was losing her.

ADRIFT

As a lecturer Professor Ord was brilliant, no one could deny that. He had a sense of timing. He could speak and judge the reaction of his audience simultaneously. His deep, resonant voice would of a sudden rise theatrically and was able to jar the mind from last night's kiss or tomorrow's tournament. This rare sense of timing, though, forsook him the moment he left the platform. In small groups his monologues were as confusing as they were dreary. Harold always found himself squirming in his chair and at last defensively suggesting a martini.

No Longer Drifting
Jackson-Britton

This, like most of Harold's remarks, Professor Ord would reject either by an annoyed frown or a firm, "No, thank you, Harold." But tonight he added, "I will have a cup of coffee, Ellen." This request caused Ellen to rise in a fluster and scurry toward the coffeemaker, and Harold was left alone facing Professor Ord and his dark, disapproving eye.

Professor Ord was handsome, but not very appealing. His posture was too straight, his dress was too fastidious, and his shrewd eyes were too accustomed to wandering from face to face to determine which, if any, really grasped the full reality of his words.

All in all, Harold didn't like him very much. It was Ellen who insisted that they entertain him. "He's lonely, she said. "Bachelors are always lonely."

Harold didn't often reflect on Ellen's motives, or, for that matter, whether or not Ellen possessed motives, but he was able to glean that she had Professor Ord mixed up in her mind with some obscure, romantic figure—like Edgar Allan Poe, more soul than flesh and blood. He consoled himself quickly, however, with the fact that Ellen had married him because he was flesh and blood—big, strong, and rugged.

"Bachelors are not lonely," he had informed her. As a bachelor, Harold had not been lonely. He could always find an agreeable companion, for to him most people were agreeable…with rare exceptions. "Ord would be great company for Socrates," he had pointed out to Ellen. "But I prefer a few beers and a football game."

Ellen, of course, with her determined enthusiasm, prevailed. Sunday night would arrive and so would Professor Ord with some amazing book he'd discovered in the library, which would turn out to be remarkably un-amazing, full of archaic ruins, weird Gothic designs, and tragic, blurry sketches from Van Gogh.

While Ord would ramble on and on, Ellen's blue eyes would widen with interest and admiration, and at times she would laugh in that surprised, breathless way of hers. Her face, sharp, alluring, was framed with glossy black curls. Harold knew other men found her attractive, but he had never really been jealous. He listened to her step from the other room and the sound of the coffee perking.

"It's very rewarding for me to meet someone like Ellen," Professor Ord was saying. "Often I start to explain something to her, and I am able to see clearly far beyond my own words. Her mind is wonderfully unlimited."

"Ellen quit a perfectly good job to take a few college courses," Harold said. "All of us can't do that."

No Longer Drifting
Jackson-Britton

"But all of us," Ord corrected, "can set aside time to expand our knowledge."

Harold, defying past experience that advised him to take no definite stand around Professor Ord, leaned closer, "I spend eight to twelve hours a day, six days a week, selling appliances. What time does that leave for all that stuff you and Ellen talk about?"

Ord's unguarded glance toward the kitchen indicated a certain lack of desire to continue with the subject. "Are you trying for a management position?"

Harold settled back in his chair. "I like everything exactly the way it is."

"I would think…" Ord's disinterested voice had floated into oblivion.

"Truth is, I turned down a chance to be assistant-manager. Did it ever occur to you that someone might want to stay right where they are?"

Ord's eyes snapped back to his. "No," he answered sharply. "Why not advance? Why not widen your circle? And keep widening it?"

"What need is there for that?" Harold answered. "Why, my boss said to me just the other day, `Harold, you could sell a TV to a blind man!'"

Harold chuckled, Professor Ord frowned, and Ellen came back into the room with the coffee. She returned, Harold thought, just in time for them to avoid open confrontation.

No Longer Drifting
Jackson-Britton

Ord resumed his discussion with Ellen precisely where it had been interrupted. All during coffee they talked about how Venice was sinking into the sea. Harold drank in hostile silence, then got up and switched on the TV.

"You could at least be polite!" Ellen faced him after Professor Ord had left.

"No one was talking to me."

"You were rude!"

Harold shrugged.

"Martin Ord is a good friend of mine! And this just happens to be my home, too!"

"*Our* home," Harold countered. "And he is no longer welcome here!"

"That's about your level!"

"What is that supposed to mean?" Harold felt a flush rise to his face. "Are you saying that I don't measure up to your professor?"

Ellen snatched empty cups from the coffee table.

"Maybe you and Ord should go live in a library."

"Maybe!" Not once glancing toward him, Ellen hurried into the kitchen.

Harold wanted to follow her. He wanted to force her to say that she preferred him to Professor Ord. But he didn't. He remained seated in the recliner and glared at the TV.

* * *

No Longer Drifting
Jackson-Britton

Next Sunday came with no mention of the weekly visitor. In spite of taking note of Ellen's certain change of attitude toward him, Harold felt satisfied that the matter with Ord was concluded and that Ellen was settling back into the old routine of their lives.

But Ellen's coldness persisted. Not that she openly opposed him in any way. She cooked his meals; she laundered his clothes; she drove his mother to the supermarket on Saturdays. Yet she challenged him in greater ways—by her lack of questions concerning who or who did not come into the store, by her lack of interest in his total weekly sales, by the books she turned to almost every night after the evening meal was finished. He fancied that she still responded to him physically, or was that to be compared to the cooking and the driving his mother to the market?

All Sunday evening Ellen sat on the leather couch that Ord and she usually occupied and with a red pencil underlined long passages from a book. Monday morning in the blackened edges of the hotcakes on his plate Harold found something tangible to criticize. "You wouldn't serve these to Ord!"

Ellen threw the spatula into the sink and left the room.

* * *

No Longer Drifting
Jackson-Britton

"Good morning, Susie," Harold addressed the pert, blonde secretary of Abel's Appliance, who turned from the filing cabinet to flash him a special smile.

Harold enjoyed Susie's admiring glances, the banter, the knowledge that he could take her out. Yet he had not seen any other woman since his marriage to Ellen. Sure, the other salesmen did; his boss, the gray-headed Mr. Thompson did, but between Harold and his opportunities there always stood Ellen and the impossibility of his ever choosing to do anything to hurt her. This, he knew, was love. And love, he knew, was what was causing his growing sense of frustration.

"You look awful!"

Harold jumped quickly at the opening Susie's observation gave him. "I feel awful! Think I'm coming down with the flu. Will you tell Mr. Thompson I'm going back home?"

Just as in the back of his mind he had suspected, the house was empty. He reacted to the emptiness first with annoyance, then with panic. He drove up one street and down the other. He looked in the shopping center and in the library and at the park near the river where Ellen walked when she wanted to be alone. Finally it dawned on him that she might not have wanted to be alone. He stopped the car at the corner station and from the phone booth dialed Professor Ord's office.

No Longer Drifting
Jackson-Britton

"Professor Ord isn't here," said a youthful voice.

"When do you expect him back?"

"He might be at the Townhouse. He generally eats breakfast there. His next class is at ten-thirty."

Harold spotted Ellen and Ord through the huge glass window of the cafe. He didn't think to pull the car into the available space. He just slammed on the brakes, abandoned the vehicle, and tore through the double doors.

Soft music surrounded him, a cozy arrangement of tables, disinterested faces that didn't even bother to glance his way. Harold couldn't force his eyes to focus on anything but Ord.

When the professor saw him, he started to rise. Before he had time to fully stand, Harold gripped his shoulders. Harold hadn't realized what an advantage he had. Ord was like a child he continued to shake at will.

Ellen clutched his arm and cried, "Stop it! Harold, are you crazy? Just stop!"

Harold did let go of Professor Ord, but with a final shove of such fury that it sent both he and the chair behind him crashing to the floor. Ellen rushed to assist him. Harold swerved around the waiter who was quickly approaching, through bystanders hovering a safe distance away, and out the door. No one attempted to stop him.

No Longer Drifting
Jackson-Britton

He had no memory of getting back into his car, but he was clutching the wheel, trying to control the shaking of his hands. For over an hour he drove aimlessly, hating Professor Ord, hating himself. By this time Ord was certain to have called the police and brought charges against him. But to his surprise no police car waited at his house. The little, brick structure was as serene as ever. The inside of the house was even more serene, or was it quiet...or was totally vacant?

Harold paced around feeling the sickness he had earlier pretended. He knew before he went into the bedroom that Ellen's suitcase, her curling iron, her cosmetics, would be gone. He sank down on the bed. Ellen just had to love him! The honeymoon here in this very room couldn't have been just a ruse to mislead him.

Why wasn't Ellen satisfied? She had an easy life. Things had been fine until their daughter, Becky, had left home for that special modeling school in California. After that, at age thirty-seven, Ellen had decided to go back to school herself. Harold had not protested, even though he did not like the idea that she was establishing goals that didn't include him.

What did he know about Ellen, really? Not what she thought or how she felt. And now, because he hadn't known or hadn't cared, he was losing her!

No Longer Drifting
Jackson-Britton

* * *

Susie's call awakened him the next morning. "Harold, are you all right? Mr. Thompson said I should check. You've just never been late before. Why didn't you call in?"

"Susie, I'm...still sick."

"You'd better see a doctor. You've never sounded worse."

"I'll see Dr. Allen today."

Harold had not considered even upon realizing that Ellen had moved out that Ord and she would be together. They were not the type of people for which romantic rashness would have any appeal. He decided that Ellen must have rented a room somewhere nearby. Today he would find her and beg her to come back home. Then everything would be just as before.

Even by nightfall, even after having inquired at every available apartment building and hotel room, even after calling Ellen's parents, from Nebraska, Harold had not found her. By eight o'clock he broke his resolution not to confront Ord and found himself pounding on the professor's door.

Professor Ord wore an immaculate tweed jacket. Harold tried to shift his gaze away from the bruise that darkened his cheekbone and spread toward his eye. The discoloration added a dimension of solemn displeasure. "Come in, Harold. I've been expecting you."

No Longer Drifting
Jackson-Britton

Ord's complete control of the situation caused Harold to feel dwarfed, even foolish. He followed Ord into a brilliant room, over-decorated with statues, lamps, and pictures. "Where is she? I've got to talk to her!"

Ord shook his head. "I can't tell you where Ellen is, Harold. I don't know."

"You must know."

Ord's dark eyes held his firmly.

"I'm... sorry," Harold managed to say. "About that..." With words trailing off, Harold, without invitation, slumped into a nearby chair. He soon found himself lost in Ord's flow of words, words that seemed to have no relationship to why he was here. Ord touched upon the possibility of a man and a woman having a relationship other than romantic. He mentioned words like professional and intellectual and ended a long, hesitant, back-tracking monologue by stating something to the effect that one often blamed others when the fault was initially one's own. With that, he fell silent, his sharp, dark eyes coldly critical.

Harold hated him more than ever.

"Most people tend," Ord said with cutting directness, "to stagnate. It's a very pitiful reality. You see it everywhere, people merely going through the motions, sleeping, working, sleeping, people doped on alcohol, on drugs or TV. Year after year they never plan, never grow."

"What's that got to do with Ellen and me?"

Ord turned curtly and lifted a stack of papers from his desk. "I can't talk to you, Harold. I simply cannot. I think you must deliberately try to be obtuse."

Harold, feeling totally defeated, drove back to his brick house on Sheldon Street. Without turning on the TV, he sank down in his favorite chair. Without Ellen there wasn't any reason to be here; there wasn't any reason to be anywhere.

Harold tried to sort out of Professor Ord's wandering stream of words some weakness he could use in his own behalf. But, Ord, in his rambling, confusing way, had left him defenseless. He rose, as if in rebellion, grabbed the dictionary and looked up the word obtuse.

"Not having an acute impression, insensitive."

The word *obtuse* seemed to stick in his mind. He found himself thinking about it and using the word in his conversations. "Thompson is being obtuse," he told Susie at work the next day. She looked up from her computer, startled.

Three long, lonely days passed before he located Ellen, then it was not through his efforts, but because of Susie. "I didn't know Ellen had quit Kay's Fashions," she said.

"You know more about her work than I do," Harold muttered. "Where did you see her?"

"In Banamaker Hall, the admissions office."

That afternoon, convincing Mr. Thompson of a relapse of the flu, Harold headed toward the university. He didn't know what to do. He simply had to see her, but he realized that any amount of pleading was not going to accomplish her return. He walked around hallways, passing groups of boisterous students, pausing before bulletin boards, trying to gather nerve enough to approach the office window. He warned himself that he must not do what she expected him to do. He would talk to her as he would any girl, any very pretty girl, he were just meeting.

Harold squared his shoulders and strode directly toward her. "I would like a catalogue of classes," he said.

Ellen's eyes widened, but she gave no other sign that she recognized him. She quickly placed a catalogue in front of him. He stood looking at her, totally incapable of following his own stern direction and walking away. "When does second semester start?"

"It has started," Ellen answered formally. "It began January l4th. It will cost you ten dollars extra for late enrollment."

He placed the catalogue on the battered wooden ledge that separated them and with his heart pounding strangely, flipped through pages. What class was it Ord had wanted Ellen to enroll in? He suddenly recalled and said, "I think I'm interested in taking Art History 312."

* * *

Harold made certain he took a seat in the crowded auditorium where Ellen could not help noticing him. He tried to avoid looking at her, and when he did, it was a sly glance that could not be observed.

At times to his surprise, he would find himself caught up in Professor Ord's lecture. The deep, precision-timed voice, with its great range, could not be evaded; neither could the sharp eyes that sought him out and seemed to talk to him directly. All of what Ord said, Harold did not by any means understand. Then he would sneak a look toward Ellen, cool, beautiful, pen poised over her notebook. She understood. So did the kids. Teenagers with glasses and blue jeans leaned forward in their chairs and crowded around the professor after each lecture.

Harold did not try to talk to Ellen. She would have expected that. He did find out by following her at a distance that she was rooming with a graduate student named Doris Anville at the top floor of a weather-beaten structure as old as the grim, limestone walls of the university buildings. But he did not try to see her.

No Longer Drifting
Jackson-Britton

Harold knew people—his neighbors, their relatives, and employees of Abel's Appliance—were beginning to ask questions. He allowed none of this to pressure him into action.

Often he left Ord's class thinking of some of the more impressive slides and feeling that Ord's talk dealt with beauty and truth and a lot of things he had never thought much about. These subjects began to appear to have something to do with his own life. He read through the assigned pages of the forty dollar book he had purchased from the college book store, and was elated by Ord's comment on his first paper, "Good thinking, Harold!"

At the next class Ord announced that the three students with the highest scores on the next test would go with him to the Nelson Art Museum in Kansas City, expenses paid. Harold's heart leaped. He pictured the professor, Ellen, and himself ambling through the museum. Ellen was impressed by his knowledgeable, yet breezy remarks on periods, styles, and theories of art. Ellen was proud of him, listening to his comments more often than to Ord's.

Harold vowed he would score among the top three. The test existed as a horizon to him, like planning for Christmas, like winning Ellen back! He set the first goal he had set in a very long time.

No Longer Drifting
Jackson-Britton

Harold began preparing at once. Every night he read until after midnight. On Friday he was interrupted by a knock. Susie stood smiling at him.

"Hi," she said. "We're having a little blow-out down at Jordan's. I thought since Ellen's not here..."

Harold took note of the golden sweater, sizes too tight, and the tan slacks that showed off long, graceful legs. Susie's hair, unlike Ellen's, hung past her shoulders. Blonde hair, or rather tan, like her slacks. His girl friends, somehow, had never been blondes like Ellen. All of them had short, black hair—dark eyes.

"We'll have to stop on the way and get some drinks," Susie was saying.

Susie wanted him. She always had. He could read desire in her eyes whenever she looked at him. Nothing now to stop them. Ellen had packed and left and that freed him.

Harold's eyes traveled over her and came to rest on the thick volume, which lay on the coffee table. "I can't tonight, Suz," he said. "I've got a class at seven-thirty."

"Harold, you're kidding! What class?"

He lifted the book with the picture of Michelangelo's David on the cover. "Art History," he said loudly.

"You going to be an artist or something?"

"I'm going to…" He stopped abruptly. "You know, expand my mind."

Susie laughed. Tan hair tossed back. Open mouth showed trim, white teeth. "Oh, brother!" she said. "You did see Dr. Allen, didn't you?"

A flush spread to Harold's face. He didn't know whether it was from embarrassment or irritation. He tried to explain. "Art…he started. "Susie, you just can't live without art. Truth and beauty, you know. They're related."

"Sure they are." Susie gazed at him oddly for a time, then said. "Think I'll run along."

She hadn't waited for him to finish speaking. Sullenly Harold finished reading the chapter on Byzantine Art. He dressed carefully for class. Pleased with the results, he stepped back from the mirror and thought of what a contrast he was to the other students with their rebelliously long hair, their faded, patched clothing. He was Martin Ord's equal!

Harold didn't understand a thing Ord said during the lecture. He should have gone to the beer party.

"Art is a reaction to the multiplying complexities and traumatic experiences of living," Ord said in a manner beyond questioning. "I want you to notice." He tapped on the screen with the pointer he always held throughout his lectures, and then he outlined the head and figure of a woman. "Here in this very painting one can clearly detect a struggle between the neo-Classicist and the Romantics."

If any struggle existed, Harold didn't see it. The professor's voice grew faint as Harold's thoughts drifted away. He had made the wrong decision enrolling in Ord's class. He should have just gone to Ellen and demanded that she return home.

Ord's voice with a dramatic change of volume again commanded his attention. This slide concerned Byzantine Art. Why does he jump from century to century? Wasn't it hard enough to follow in sequence? Harold wasn't absorbing any of the points he made and hoped it was all in the text so he could score high on the test. The test—it was beginning to be all he thought about!

Harold was the first one to leave the auditorium after class was dismissed. Concealed from view by the position of the huge cement fountain and by the thickness of trees, he sat on a bench, leaning forward, so he could keep the doorway in view.

Crowds of youth, worries closed with books, flooded from the auditorium. Time passed. The kids quit coming out. Perhaps he had missed Ellen in the rush. He rose and started crossing toward the sidewalk when he saw them, Professor Ord and Ellen.

He edged back into the trees. He could hear Ord talking—words like proportion and concept of beauty and vertical balance. Ellen, intrigued, did not look right or left. Harold had difficulty breathing. His breath wanted to come too quickly, too loudly.

They strolled straight toward Ord's wine-colored car. Harold clutched his fists. He forced himself not to take a step toward them. He stood frozen as Ord open the door for Ellen and as he watched them drive away.

Harold raced to his own car. He wouldn't harm Ellen. This wasn't her fault. Ord had hypnotized her. But, Ord, he was going to kill with his bare hands!

From a distance Harold followed the lights of Ord's car paced ever so slowly around the curving lanes of the campus. Ord took a right at Banamaker Hall.

Ord quickly assisted Ellen from his car and they walked toward her door. Before Harold had pulled his car to a stop, Ord was back in his vehicle and driving away. Not much there to motivate murder.

* * *

Harold rose early the next morning and arrived at the store just as Mr. Thompson was unlocking the door. He said a little belligerently, "I want the assistant managership. If I don't get it, I'm looking for another job."

"Is that what's been bothering you?"

"Nothing's bothering me. I've just stayed in one place much too long. It's time I advanced."

No Longer Drifting
Jackson-Britton

"Those were my words to you over a year ago. In fact," Mr. Thompson added, "when I retire, I want you to take over."

"I will," Harold said firmly, momentarily forgetting all his fears of added responsibility.

In fact, Harold thought of nothing but the art history test. He studied until he could give names, dates, titles, artists. He could recognize styles—Classical, Romanesque, Rococo. He had read the thick volume through and reread parts, committing to memory those sentences he did not fully comprehend. The test, which he equated with getting Ellen back, was tomorrow!

Harold didn't sleep that night. He'd keep waking up, prowling through the lonely house, drinking coffee or eating peanut-butter sandwiches.

Once settled in bed again, he would begin thinking about art. He couldn't for the life of him remember whether Houdon sculptured Voltaire or Voltaire sculptured Houdon. He got up and flipped through the book.

"Hudson's sculpture depicts rather the worldly-wise and even tolerant expression of a man who at the end of his life appears garbed in the robes of ancient Roman republicanism."

No Longer Drifting
Jackson-Britton

Voltaire wasn't a Roman, or was he? Damn! He got a copy of the world book and looked up Voltaire. By morning he was exhausted.

Harold didn't know how he did on the test. He knew he wrote something down for every slide. He knew, too, that the slides came and went with merciless rapidity. Some of them he knew with confidence. Some of the information blurred in his mind and he groped at the answers with frantic confusion.

Ord gathered the papers immediately after the last slide, saying, "I'll hand these back Friday."

Friday approached slowly. Harold's vision of Ellen hearing his name as winner grew to become a reality in his mind. Friday night Harold dressed slowly, pressing his blue suit, adding an extra splash of Ellen's favorite after-shave.

Promptly on the dot of seven, Ord, papers in hand, stepped to center stage. In a voice that resounded throughout the auditorium, he announced, "Ellen Douglas won first place with a score of 98%. No one has ever surpassed this mark in my many years as professor." Ord beamed. "Excellent job, Ellen!"

The crowd clapped. Harold because everyone else was looking at Ellen, looked at her himself. Her face was bright and glowing with happiness. She smiled modestly as Ord walked down the steps, down the aisle, and handed her exam to her.

"Second place is—Martha Davis! Martha's score is 90%. Congratulations, Martha."

Everyone applauded as the girl with the braces on her teeth let out a shriek.

Harold's mouth went dry. His heart pounded loudly. He had sat forward in the chair and clutched the seat in front of him.

"Third place. Quite a drop from first, but still remarkably good--83%. Bill Remington! Bill."

Bill Remington, a kid with a prominent Adam's apple and rimless glasses jumped to his feet. No! Harold had to have at least come in third! Everything depended on his winning!

Ord walked around calling names. At last he approached Harold. "You must have been a little nervous, Harold. Maybe next time."

Sixty-seven, a very low C! Harold skimmed the red marks scattered over the paper, his eyes locking on the long, crimson minus after the C. Below average! That's what he was, at best. Below average!

Ord leaned elegantly forward, concern showing on the shrewd, intense features. The dark eyes, not unkind, remained on Harold. "This is probably the first timed test you've taken in years. You did very well, I'd say!" He smiled encouragingly. "Yes, good. Good work!"

Ord went on walking from person to person. "Thornton, Kreiger, Andrews."

Harold wiped his hand over his face. Sweat made his palms moist. He felt like a fool. He was a fool! People were looking at him. Ellen was looking at him. Had everyone in the room stopped everything to stare at him?

Harold crushed the exam paper into a wad and strode from the auditorium. He didn't feel physically able to drive home. He headed for the bench beside the fountain and sank down. He stared hopelessly at the ground.

"Harold." He hadn't seen Ellen approach. Her voice sounded calm and gentle. She seated herself on the bench beside him. He didn't look at her.

"It's only a test," she said matter-of-factly. "There are three more before the final."

"I'm not likely to do any better...ever," Harold said. "Ord was right." His voice rose with conviction. "I'm not good enough for you!"

Ellen didn't speak.

"I want you to divorce me!"

Out of the corner of his eye he could see her profile—a beautiful, classic image topped with black curls stirring slightly with the gusts of wind.

No Longer Drifting
Jackson-Britton

"I don't want a divorce, Harold. I love you."

Harold sat in stony silence. "How could you love me? I can barely pass Art History!"

Ellen laughed. When he turned to look at her, he recognized in her eyes the old glint of admiration.

No Longer Drifting
Jackson-Britton

Jessie learns it is never too late to follow your dreams.

THE PEACOCK ON THE SHELF

Silver earrings flashed against snow-white curls as Theda Cooper slid the steel walker on to the next tier of stone steps. "Twenty-eight, twenty-nine—"Jessie, a few steps behind her, mentally counted. She always kept her fingers crossed until her friend reached the entrance to the church. Frost made the steps icy; last winter Theda had fallen and broken her hip, and now she had to use the walker instead of a cane.

"Why does she insist on coming out in weather like this?" Jessie read anxiousness and a touch of pity in her husband's voice. "The pastor said he'd tape her the sermons," he added, genuinely puzzled. "Why, she wouldn't even have to get out of bed."

"That's not Theda's way," Jessie replied, accustomed to defending her to Roy.

Roy shrugged. "But look at her. She's getting so frail. Why, it's all she can do to make it up the church steps."

"And yet she never misses a Sunday." As always, the woman's iron-clad determination awed Jessie. At the same time, the irony of it saddened her. The same stubborn will that had taken driven Theda to travel to major art shows and museums all over the world could now barely carry her as far as the community church just down the block from her home.

Children in their Sunday best frolicked by. Men and women, assuming hurried expressions, bypassed the congestion on the stairs. Theda's slowness caused all three of them to move at a snail's pace.

"She'll probably end up in the old folk's home before the winter's through," Roy said, and his fatalistic tone made Jessie shiver.

"Not if I know Theda," Jessie replied, but the wind blew her words back to her.

Theda had been a part of Jessie's life for as long as she could remember. As a child, Jessie had been a frequent visitor to Theda's old house on the corner across from the church. Even then, Theda's thick coil of hair had been frosted with white. Whenever Jessie and her mother dropped by, Theda would brew her special tea, filling the house with the smell of spice while she showed them her newest painting.

Theda lived for art! Within that huge museum of a house were rare paintings and marble sculptures. The glass cabinets displayed a wealth of treasure Theda had brought back from her travels in Europe, India, and the Orient.

Theda had encouraged five-year-old Jessie practice painting upon her expensive easel, experimenting with rainbow shades of colors.

"I only dabble at the canvas. But I love art—that's why I have always surrounded myself with beautiful things. They are a source of joy to me."

Theda had let Jessie's small hands hold the treasures she had collected through the years—the tiny, hand-painted flowers on silk, the dainty China teacups, the fragile Dresden figurines.

"Careful, Jessie," her mother was always whispering nervously, behind Theda's back. "I'm afraid you might break something."

The day she discovered the peacock, Jessie forgot her mother's warning. Her eyes were fastened to the high top shelf where Theda kept the glass *birdie*. In frustration, she strained to reach it, but the shelf was too high.

Later, while her mother and Theda were visiting, she had pulled over a kitchen chair. But the object of her desire was still far out of reach. As she stretched her arms upward, she suddenly lost her balance and fell. The chair came toppling over, sprawling Jessie upon the floor. Jessie began to cry.

Her mother had been upset and embarrassed, but Theda had only smiled. She reached high above Jessie's head and brought down the prized treasure for her— the delicate crystal peacock with paper-thin, fanned tail. Jessie could still remember the feel of that precious object cradled in her hands.

As a young girl of twelve, Jessie remembered lying on Theda's plush Persian rug with a stack of travel magazines spread out beside her. While the two women had talked, she had traced out imaginary routes to Paris and Rome, where the gypsy in her had taken Theda. Jessie hungered to see these places for herself, as Theda had done. Every once in a while, she would tug her mother's leg, demanding, "Why can't we go there? Let's go to France this summer!"

Her mother had only rolled her eyes. "Where are we going to find the time? Where are we going to get the money?"

No Longer Drifting
Jackson-Britton

"Well, I'm going someday!" Jessie had insisted. "When I become a famous artist, I'll study in Paris!"

"Paris!" Her mother had laughed. "You're such a dreamer, Child! I don't know where you get those flighty ideas of yours."

But Theda had not laughed. For eighth grade graduation, she had given Jessie her first set of paints. Many times after that, Jessie had come to Theda's house. Often, the two of them would set up their easels together and paint the mountains outside the window. Sometimes they would take long walks in the woods, bringing home flowers for the table and new ideas for the canvas. In this small, white-haired woman, Jessie had found an ally, someone to acknowledge her innermost dreams.

During the next three years, Jessie's painting grew and blossomed. "That's nice," her boyfriend, Roy, would comment politely when she showed him the shadowed canvasses that reflected the depths of her soul. But the absence of a certain light in his eyes told her that her passion for art was something he would never be able to fully share.

It was to Theda Jessie brought first the exciting news about being accepted for an international fellowship to study at the Sorbonne in Paris.

No Longer Drifting
Jackson-Britton

"I feel like I'm being pulled in two directions at once," Jessie confided. "Roy hasn't said anything, but I know he doesn't want me to go."

"You have a great talent. It would be a shame to let it go to waste," Theda had advised her.

Jessie considered her deepening relationship with Roy.

As if reading her thoughts, Theda said, "You should never have to choose between someone you love and something that is so important to you."

But Theda had been wrong. That evening, over candlelit dinner, Roy had given her the diamond ring. "Maybe I'm being selfish but I don't want you to go, Jessie. Please stay here with me while I work on establishing the business...our future."

Two years was a long time to be apart. Jessie studied Roy's handsome, serious face and knew she could not take the chance on losing him.

In the end, Jessie turned down the opportunity to study at the Sorbonne. The chance, once refused, had never come again. Jessie helped Roy in the law firm. Then the kids had come, pleasures and problems piled on top of each other like sandbags. Time, she told herself, I could never find enough time to resume painting. Through the years, she harbored vague dreams of returning to her artwork, but the easel remained shoved to the back of the garage, collecting dust. The sight of it always caused a painful, empty feeling in her heart.

It became more and more easy to bury her private dreams until those early aspirations seemed as far out of reach as the peacock on the shelf had once been. Gradually, she had visited Theda less and less until the once strong tie of friendship threatened to loosen its knots and silently slip away.

In fact, Jessie hadn't realized how long it had been since she had really talked to Theda until the accident last winter. After Theda's fall, she had gone to help her. Theda had insisted on her bringing the old easel close to the bed so that she could finish a mountain scene she had been working on. Just like the old days, the two of them talked about art and painting and travel.

Theda's last trip had been to Italy. "Can you believe that I climbed up to the top of the Tower of Pisa?" She gave a little laugh. "I was the oldest one in the tour group. None of the others thought I would make it."

"I'll never forget those last few steep, crooked steps that led up to the bell tower." She looked at Jessie, her clear, blue eyes reflecting the colors of her bright, flowered robe. "You know, I've always been glad I made that climb. I believe I saw the entire world from the top of that bell tower."

No Longer Drifting
Jackson-Britton

"I guessed I missed my opportunity to see the world," Jessie said quietly. "Oh, I'm not sorry that I chose to stay and marry Roy. But a part of me always regretted that I missed my chance to go to Paris and study."

"Paris doesn't make the artist!" Theda pressed a hand to her heart. "It's something inside here, some silent calling that cannot be ignored. Travel was my way. But we all take different paths."

"Sometimes I regret giving up on my painting," Jessie said wistfully.

"Why, then, have you settled for less?"

"I guess I just don't have your drive and ambition." One kind of fear had kept Jessie from going on that trip; another had made her quit her painting entirely. It was as if by depriving herself of this pleasure, she might become a better wife and mother. "It got too difficult. Finally, I just gave up."

"Or maybe you simply weren't ready." Theda's hand gestured toward the China cabinet and she said with a smile, "Remember when you were little, and you wanted the peacock?"

Jessie nodded. "It seemed the most important thing in the world to me then."

"Get it down for me."

Jessie had grown to be a tall woman; she did not even have to stretch to reach the peacock now.

Obediently, she had taken it down from the high shelf that day and held it out to Theda.

When Jessie began to paint again, she felt like something that had been dying in her soul had taken root and sprung back to life. When dinner became later each night, when she asked Roy to spend more time with the children, his silent accusations punished more than harsh words. She felt tense and uneasy when, late one evening, she heard his footsteps pause in the hallway.

Roy entered the spare room she had converted into a studio and approached the easel. For a long time he stood quietly studying the snow swept scene upon the canvas. When he turned back to Jessie, he looked sad and a little bewildered. "I can't pretend to understand art, but I can see that you have a special talent. I never intended to take anything away from you, Jessie. I know you need to do what it takes to make you happy."

Jessie remembered Theda's pride in her when she told her about that first art show scheduled for April. Jessie watched Theda, her mentor, now so frail and slow. The voluminous folds of the camelhair coat seemed to swallow her up. Theda Cooper tottered a little as she reached the last step. Jessie rushed to offer her aid, but a firm hand gently declined. Jessie swallowed hard. In her heart she knew Theda might not even be here in the spring.

No Longer Drifting
Jackson-Britton

She remembered how Theda's thin, white hands had closed over hers the day she had insisted she take the peacock. "Keep it," she had told her, "somewhere within easy sight. To remind you that dreams are never too far out of reach."

Paul, young and grief-stricken, needed a friend. He needed the help of Freddie Ames. Or did he?

WHERE IS FREDDIE NOW?

Paul's father lay dead in the coffin, his mother in shock at St. Mary's Hospital. Paul had rushed home from college, his whole mind and soul perfectly split in two. One part of him—so strong, so sane—saw to the arrangements; comforted Mother; took over each detail of the household, the hospital, Dad's massive business interests. The other side of him—the real Paul O'Hara—was so mortally hurt that his very being hung isolated somewhere beyond hope or consolation.

"It's a road we all must travel," Rev. Murray said.

Yes, Paul thought, death must befall the old, the sick, the stagnant, but not someone vital, handsome, wise, someone in the very prime of life. Paul's gaze fell to the waxen face of his father, then his eyes, dry, brittle, hard to focus, raised, skimmed the room for Freddie Ames. All evening he had looked for Freddie. However hard it was for Paul to admit it, he needed Freddie's support or at least his presence, an alliance of mutual grief. Because of Freddie's place of honor in Dad's life, he should be here now, beside Paul, the only child.

Paul had been at the funeral home since seven, uncomfortable in the hard bench, rising woodenly to supply an answer or shake someone's hand. Exhaustion now made his shoulders ache, his headache. The boy he was such a short time ago tried to break into his awful solitude and demand tears to express his anguish. To assuage his grief, he hated all the hundreds and hundreds of people Dad had helped, so generously and freely, most of whom weren't showing up now to pay him tribute. He hated, in particular, Freddie Ames, who hadn't even bothered to stop by the house.

Dad's shadow. Wherever Dad was, Freddie followed—the favorite son, who wasn't a son at all. Freddie benefited from the relationship that should have been Paul's. Paul had been usurped, left an intruder, an outsider, a son without a father. Last summer Dad had hit Paul with the final blow; he had taken Freddie as his business partner in O'Hara's Mercantile.

"I don't want to finish college," Paul had opposed. "The store belongs to the O'Hara's. Remember what Grandfather told me, 'father to son, father to son.' I grew up in the store. Make me your partner. I want the partnership!"

"My business is conservative," Dad had chuckled. "And you, Paul, are your mother's son."

"I want my share of O'Hara's Mercantile more than I want anything else. Grandfather understood. Why don't you?"

Dad had understood; all the same, he had established Freddie Ames as his one and equal partner.

Paul glanced at Dad's face. Dad took so much stock in Freddie, his opinions, his feelings. He spent years worrying about Freddie's losses, the death of Freddie's only child, Freddie's unhappy marriage.

Where is Freddie now? Paul wanted to jump to his feet and scream the words, but Dad hadn't heard him in life and certainly wasn't going to hear him now.

"I'll get even with Freddie!" Paul vowed as he left the funeral home. "I'll make him sorry he wasn't here to help me!"

By the next morning Paul's hatred and resolve had mellowed and he settled on the mere act of asking Freddie to do his duty. He stopped by the smart, brick house Dad had financed for the Ames' and found Freddie in the basement. Freddie rubbed oil on a small gun he had taken from the overflowing gun-cabinet. He barely looked up.

Paul had never seen Freddie without Dad. At the sight of Freddie, Paul was stricken by a sense of loss. Dad really was dead! He'd never again hear the bellowing laughter, the teasing voice. A shaking started in Paul's legs. He stopped to brace his hand against a workbench. The sense of loss magnified, became tinged with a childish jealousy.

"Where were you last night?"

Freddie's guarded, black eyes retreated from Paul's stare. "I was here."

"I thought you'd surely be..." Paul didn't go on.

Freddie reached for some sandpaper and slowly sanded rust from the blue-black barrel. Paul saw only lank, black hair and shadows from the overhead light.

"Maybe you'll drop by the hospital today."

Freddie's long hand slid faster and faster up and down the barrel.

"I thought I'd keep Mother there until after the funeral."

Freddie's black eyes, more dominant for the thinness of jaw line, rose again, blank and opaque.

No Longer Drifting
Jackson-Britton

Paul hadn't expected Freddie to be calm, placid. Not about Dad's death! Paul felt a reeling start in his head. The bastard! Paul thought. He doesn't even care!

"Mother's taking this very hard," Paul voice sounded choked, far away. "You can't imagine how hard. She may never recover."

Freddie lifted a small rod from the table and slid it into the gun barrel.

Paul whirled around and started to the door.

"She'll be all right," Freddie said. "Don't worry."

"I'm going to see her now." Paul, hand on the doorknob, looked back entreatingly. "Maybe you'd like to come along."

"I can't," Freddie said. "I can't get away now."

Freddie didn't get away for Tom O'Hara's funeral either. Gloria, Freddie's wife, so pale and beautiful in black, wept alone at the back of the church. She wouldn't have cried at all, Paul thought, had she known what Dad always said about her. "Little tart," he would roar. "Don't know why Freddie puts up with her."

At the graveyard after the service Gloria hugged Paul tightly. She kept clinging to him, wet cheek against his, thick strands of blonde hair dangling across his mouth. The smell of strong perfume blending with the odor of flowers half-sickened him.

No Longer Drifting
Jackson-Britton

"You're just the picture of Tom!" she cried. "You're so big and strong. You look just exactly like him!"

Everyone always referred to their looking alike, no one to their being alike. Paul should have, he thought, inherited more—more of the insight, the scope, the generous good-will.

When Freddie didn't show up for work either Monday or Tuesday, Paul stopped by his house again.

"He left this morning early. I thought he was going to the store," Gloria said. "Hey, why don't you come in and wait for him? I've just made some cinnamon rolls."

Embarrassed. He was always embarrassed around the Ames'. Paul stood awkwardly by the stove as Gloria took the pan from the oven and set it on the bar.

Gloria would have to be nearing forty, but she looked like a high school girl. Today she wore skimpy shorts and a halter that revealed far too much of the pure white skin.

Paul's eyes lingered on her body, so full, smooth and soft, then he looked away, stepped back and sank down on the couch.

"How's college?" Gloria reached up to unclip her hair. Blond curls fell around her full face.

"I'm not going back. I've quit. To run the store."

No Longer Drifting
Jackson-Britton

"Bet your mom will be glad." Gloria's eyes darted to a picture of Dad and Freddie that hung over the desk. "I can't imagine you and Freddie being partners."

Paul accepted the cinnamon roll. Gloria replaced the platter on the bar and sat beside him on the couch. Her nearness made his heart pound.

"How could someone be so handsome," she said huskily. "And not even know it!"

The roll, hot and moist in his hand, turned dry and hard in his mouth. Paul remembered last summer at the lake when everyone else had gone out on the boat. He recalled swimming away from Gloria, flashes of brilliant sun half-blinding him. What sort of a fool had he been to run away from her? He had never met anyone so beautiful.

The roll was gone. Self-consciously, Paul stared at his hands, large, sunburnt. Then he stood up quickly.

Gloria rose at the same time. Both arms slipped around his neck. He felt the pressure of her body against his. Freddie won't be back for hours, he thought. For a while he could find pleasure, forgetfulness.

"I've always wanted us to be alone like this," she said.

And it wasn't as if he were trying to seduce her. Gloria was doing the inviting.

No Longer Drifting
Jackson-Britton

Paul drew her even closer. His lips brushed against hers; she moaned as they moved to her bare neck. Freddie had taken everything from him. Now he would take something from Freddie!

The malignancy of his thoughts caused him to pull away. My God, what sort of a person was he becoming? Paul let go of her so abruptly that she staggered a little to keep her balance.

"Paul, it's okay. Freddie won't be back. Not for a long time."

"I...I've got to get to the store."

"Please, Paul, don't leave! Paul!"

* * *

On Thursday Paul leaned on the balcony railing and watched customers scanning merchandise. O'Hara's Mercantile, a store with pride—a general store, a community store started by his great-grandfather in 1872, two years after the town was founded.

Why had Dad wanted Freddie as a partner in O'Hara's Mercantile instead of him? Had it gone beyond the clear fact that Dad really loved Freddie more than he loved his own son? Maybe Freddie actually did surpass him. Paul noticed the way his employees shielded their skepticism behind polite smiles and courteous obedience, not acknowledging him as boss. Was that only because he must seem so very young to them, so very much at a loss?

Paul's damp hands tightened on the balcony railing. He could almost hear the sound of Dad's endless banter drifting up to him. He could hear his booming laughter, see the pleasant ease with which Dad and Freddie exchanged talk and task.

What had Dad, so earthy, so fun-loving, seen in Freddie Ames, in someone so impalpable? Freddie seldom even smiled, only that stretching of thin lips in some reserved appreciation of Dad's hearty, Irish humor.

Freddie was Paul's partner now. A fact he must live with. Freddie was important to O'Hara's Mercantile, more important than Paul O'Hara would ever be. Customers looked for Freddie, needing his quiet manner, his knowledgeable air.

Paul had often watched the customers around Freddie, had seen a slight word from Freddie bring hands to billfolds. They trusted Freddie to be honest, close, conservative; they allowed themselves, as Dad had, to fall under his influence.

Why, Paul didn't know. Freddie wasn't even likeable. Sometimes he deliberately ignored everyone. Sometimes he was around, only like some unwilling presence.

No Longer Drifting
Jackson-Britton

Bitterly Paul stalked into his dad's office and sank down in his chair, eyes avoiding the huge oil painting of Dad and Freddie set against the backdrop of the hardware store. Paul's sudden intrusion into management, his lack of experience, for a moment overwhelmed him. He didn't know what to do or even how to begin. The truth loomed before him: he must lean on Freddie, learn from Freddie, depend on Freddie! Damn it all! He needed Freddie's help!

Paul reached for the phone and waited a long time for Freddie's voice, "What is it?"

"You've got to help out," Paul said. "Can you come down to the store?"

A hesitation. "There are things I have to see to."

"I've got to talk to you. Right away. Now!" He slammed down the receiver.

Paul waited impatiently, his eye on the main entrance. Freddie stopped several times to engage in some brief, stoic exchange of words, first with Sue at the cash register, then with customers as he proceeded with solemn dignity toward the stairway. Freddie hadn't shown up at all to help Mother. He hadn't shown up when Paul needed him at the funeral. But here he was. Didn't that reveal where Freddie's loyalties lay—with himself, with profit and loss!

Stirrings of anger rose as Paul stepped forward to meet him. Paul had made the phone call impulsively, but Freddie was a man who had to be addressed on an intellectual level. Paul groped for shreds of logic, for justification.

Freddie's large dark eyes stared at him soberly. "What do you want that can't wait?"

"I have," Paul said ardently, "lots of ideas about the store. I want..." He waved his hand a bit frantically. "I want to expand the store! I want to get a line of electronics." Several customers were glancing at the balcony toward them. Paul battled to control the volume of his voice. "TV's, stereos, video rentals! That's where the money is!"

"Is that all you wanted?"

"You're afraid of change! Our business has to change, to grow!"

Freddie met Paul's raving with a passionless composure. The gap, always between them, grew wider. Without a word, Freddie turned and started back down the steps.

"Wait! My ideas at least deserve an answer."

"An electronics line won't go over here."

A stock clerk holding a pad approached them. He looked only at Freddie. "Shall I double the order on paint?"

"Yes." Freddie seemed absorbed in matters not at hand. "Triple the white."

No Longer Drifting
Jackson-Britton

"You're not just going to walk out. We've got things to talk about."

Freddie started to turn away. Paul reached out to detain him, but Freddie slipped away from his clutching fingers as if he were a ghost with no substance or feeling.

Once Freddie was outside, Paul pounced after him. "So you don't like me. I can live with that."

Freddie remained unresponsive.

"You don't want to work with me, that's it, isn't it?" How could Dad ever have liked him? Paul had never met anyone so cold, so uncaring. "Ok. I'm willing to pay for your share of the store."

Freddie said nothing.

Paul grew more and more inflamed by not being taken seriously. "I'll give you what it's worth. I'll give you twice what it's worth!"

Freddie stopped and looked at him. The distance between them grew even greater, became frigid.

"Just name the price! Say something, damn it! I want an answer. Are you going to sell out to me?"

Freddie spoke just one word. "No."

Blood rushed to Paul's face. He struggled to keep his hands loose at his sides. "I'll tell you one thing, if you're going to be my partner, you had damn well better start acting like one!"

With the same detachment, Freddie slid in under the wheel and started the motor of his car.

"I'll expect you to be here at eight o'clock in the morning!" Paul yelled after him.

* * *

Paul had not slept well. Mother, listless in her pale robe, sat by the door where she would sit all day. The sight of her, the cup after cup of black coffee, had made him slightly ill.

The silent store looked different in the early morning. Paul listened to the uneven clack of his footsteps across the oak floor, on the metal steps.

As he passed Freddie's office, he stepped back to glance inside. He saw Freddie's back, clad in a white shirt, slumped across the desk. He'd never got along with Gloria; everyone knew that. He must have slept here last night.

"Freddie."

The form didn't stir.

Paul drew nearer. He reached out to touch the shoulder. As he did, his gaze shifted to the lank, dark hair covered with blood. Blood lay in a pool on the edge of the desk and had begun to drip onto the gray carpet.

Paul's hands snapped back; his fingers clutched his own jacket. "No! Oh, God, no!"

No Longer Drifting
Jackson-Britton

The small gun, carefully polished, gleamed blue-black. It lay limp in Freddie's long fingers.

Horrified, Paul backed away. Coffee overflowed in his throat. He ran to the bathroom sink. Afterwards he splashed water on his face and sobbed into his wet hands.

Shaken, but able to push buttons on the phone, he called for help. As Paul replaced the receiver, his eyes locked on the painting above Dad's desk—Dad, grinning, Freddie beside him, remote, unsmiling, but there, always there. Freddie, so very, very important.

Dad's image seemed to vanish from the picture. Freddie stood alone; dark eyes stared at Paul, and Paul understood their depth, their loneliness.

"Freddie," he said to the painted eyes. "I needed your help! I really did!"

The eyes, like in life, remained impassive.

No Longer Drifting
Jackson-Britton

Janine really didn't have time for this party with Mom. She couldn't wait to get back to her own friends and her own life.

THE MANTEL CLOCK

"Are you coming over this afternoon?" Janine's mother asked.

"Oh, Mom. I told you not to go to any trouble for my birthday this year!" "Besides," Janine protested, "I've already made plans for this afternoon with some of my friends."

"Can't you just drop by for a few minutes?" her mother persisted. "I made chocolate cake with white icing—your favorite!"

Janine weighed spending an afternoon with her mother against the day she had planned. All of her new college friends would be at Nicole's house. She would rather go there, but a sense of family duty, and a sudden weakening at the thought of a slice of Mom's homemade chocolate cake, made her give in. "All right. I guess I could stop by."

A reluctance to leave her newfound independence behind slowed Janine's steps as she made her way over the snow-crusted walk. She was proud of having her own place, of finally breaking free from home. The cozy apartment she had fixed up and painted herself, saving money from her part-time job.

As Janine drove across town, she could imagine the cake with its birthday candles, the kitchen decorated with streamers more befitting an eight-year-old than a grown woman of eighteen.

Janine's mother had named her after the month she was born, January, and throughout her childhood she had never failed to make the cold winter day a special occasion. Janine remembered a time, all through grade school, when the *big day*, her birthday, was looked forward to with so much anticipation she could hardly sleep—the hats, the balloons, the brightly colored boxes filled with abundant presents, the stuffed animals and new, ruffled dresses.

In the past few years, since Dad had died, the annual birthday party had become a tradition she tolerated more for her mother's benefit than her own.

No Longer Drifting
Jackson-Britton

She had secretly hoped Mom would take the hint that she didn't need to go to all the bother this year.

Her mother would be upset because she had missed coming over for a while. Mom expected her to spend all of her free time with her, to drop in every weekend. Mom just couldn't understand that she had other things to do that were more important than Thursday night Bingo and Sunday night's chicken dinner. She didn't need all those extra calories, anyway. She would think up some excuse for next week and Mom would just have to accept it. She would have to face the fact that Janine wasn't a little girl anymore. She deserved a life of her own. After all, mom couldn't expect things to remain the same forever.

Mom, still wearing a flowered apron over her dress, stepped out to meet her. "It's always good to have you home," she said, hugging her close. She held her for a moment at arm's length. "It seems ages since you stopped by. Let me look at you. Is that a new haircut?"

Her words made Janine feel like a child again as she followed her mother into the pleasant, yellow house with the white shutters.

As she had so many afternoons returning from school, Janine paused to hang her jacket on the old hall tree. The room was filled with familiar memories. Dad's portrait smiled reassuringly from its place of honor above the fireplace. Janine's gaze wandered to the comfortable plaid sofa, the scattering of planters across the windowsill. Had Mom ever grown any other kind of flower but African violets?

As she stepped to warm herself by the hearth, Janine's eyes fell to the heavy antique clock, lacquered black with golden gilt trim. It seemed to have always set upon the mantel. Tick, tick, tick—how slowly time would drag today. In any event, the hour she had allowed Mom would soon be over.

Janine often wondered how she had ever lived there, amid the many restrictions, the imposition of the twelve o'clock curfew. She didn't have time for this kid-stuff any longer. She couldn't wait to get back to her own friends and her own life.

"Come into the kitchen," Mom was saying.

The cake, white icing carefully decorated with pink flowers, her name across the middle in large letters, served as the table centerpiece. And sure enough, colored streamers dangled from the chandelier. But something seemed different this year. Janine suddenly realized the change. The table was set, not for two, but for three.

"I hope you don't mind. I've invited Theodore over to join us."

"You invited Mr. Spenser to my birthday party?"

No Longer Drifting
Jackson-Britton

Theodore Spenser had been a history teacher where Janine had gone to high school, although she had never taken any of his classes. Her mother had met him through the PTA, and they had become good friends. Since Dad died, Janine knew he often came around to help her mom fix things around the house. That was fine. Maybe having him around would get Mom off of her back.

"He should be here any minute." Her mother seemed nervous as she straightened her hair.

Before Janine could ask any more questions, the doorbell rang.

"Good afternoon, Rose. You look lovely."

Having always been *Mom* to her, Janine always felt a little startled whenever she heard anyone call her mother by her given name. Now, she felt even more amazed when Mr. Spencer kissed her on the cheek.

Janine had never disliked him. In fact, his slow, mild manner and easy smile reminded her of Dad.

They followed Mom back into the kitchen. Mr. Spencer playfully pulled at the tie on her apron, undoing the bow.

"Teddy, stop!" her mother protested with a blush. As she took off the apron, Janine noticed she was wearing her nice skirt and sweater, the outfit she usually reserved for church.

No Longer Drifting
Jackson-Britton

Janine suddenly saw her as if through a stranger's eyes, an attractive woman with delicate features and a cloud of soft brown hair several shades lighter than her own. Mom was smiling. Grudgingly, Janine realized how pretty the smile made her, how seldom she had seen it since Dad had died.

"Hope I'm not intruding here." This man, who jovially insisted she call him Teddy, would always be Mr. Spencer to Janine. He immediately made himself at home, seated himself in Dad's old chair at the head of the table.

But he *was* intruding. Janine deeply resented his presence. Suddenly she realized she had a lot of things to discuss with Mom. She wanted to tell her how much she hated English Composition, and that she was considering changing her major. She wanted to ask her advice about the new guy she was seeing, and tell Mom that the speech teacher graded unfairly because he was such a jerk. But how could they talk with Mr. Spencer there, butting in?

Mom poured tea and sliced and served the cake. They ate with the clicking of forks, long silences interspersed with neutral conversation, as if they were polite strangers.

Every once in a while, she saw Mr. Spencer and her mother exchanging looks. The moist, rich taste of chocolate seemed to stick Janine's throat. Suddenly, Janine felt like the outsider.

"Why don't you open your gift now?"

This year, only one small, carefully wrapped package sat beside her plate. Janine removed the bow and white tissue paper. Inside was a rather garish watch with a wide, red band. Nothing Janine would ever wear.

"I hope you like it," Mom said, leaning forward anxiously. "Teddy helped me pick it out."

Janine hated it, would never wear it, but of course she couldn't say that. "It's just what I needed." She gave a forced smile. "It'll be perfect for school."

"You have to get to those classes on time," Mr. Spencer remarked with exaggerated enthusiasm.

Janine helped herself to another slice of cake. The room was filled with a sudden, awkward silence. Once again, she caught her mother and Theodore Spencer exchanging furtive glances. What was going on, Janine wondered.

Mom cleared her throat before speaking. "Janine, I have something to tell you." She took a deep breath. "I know this is rather sudden, but you know Teddy and I have been seeing each other for some time now."

Good. Mom needed someone besides Janine in her life. Maybe he could take Mom to Bingo instead of her, stand in for all those greasy chicken dinners.

No Longer Drifting
Jackson-Britton

"We're getting married," Mr. Spencer burst in happily, reaching for Mom's hand.

"Married?" Janine felt jolted. How could Mother even think about such a thing?

As her mother's gaze followed Janine's to Dad's portrait, visible on the wall above the mantel clock, small lines returned, adding years. Then, as if brushing the past away, Mom continued brightly, "We were thinking of a June wedding, maybe even a little honeymoon trip to Cancun."

Before Janine could fully digest this bit of news, Mom added, "I'm going to sell the house."

"Sell the house?" Janine echoed, putting down her fork. Her words fell upon dead stillness.

Sickness washed over her. Her next birthday party would not be held in this kitchen. Probably Mom wouldn't even have time to bake a cake or hang those streamers the way she always did. In an attempt to hold on to what she thought she hadn't even wanted, Janine cried, "Mom, how could you?"

"Your father and I had a wonderful life together. And I'll always miss him. But there comes a time when I have to accept what has happened."

Janine's entire childhood seemed to disappear before her eyes. Her secure world shattered as if the house had suddenly gone up in a cloud of black smoke. Everything gone, the pictures, her old room—that antique clock on the mantel that she thought would remain ticking through all eternity.

"I know this might come as a shock for you, Janine. But whether we like it or not, change is part of life. You can't expect things to stay the same forever."

What is cowardice? Jim wondered if anyone could answer that all-important question.

THE COWARD

Jim crossed the busy road that divided the run-down hotel from the park. He walked swiftly, winding around oaks that stood tall and imposing, like guards protecting the huge monument.

Already his eyes wandered down the list of Vietnam causalities: Allen, Asby, Biggert, Brogdon. His gaze slid past the last name, then back—Thomas R. Brogdon. Jim stepped closer. His hand reached out and felt the sharp-etched edges of granite. The stone was cold against his stiff fingers. Thomas R. Brogdon, hero, Jim Brogdon, coward!

No Longer Drifting
Jackson-Britton

His kid brother's face materialized surrounded by gray stone flecked with silver. Tommy's wide mouth with the ever-present grin, the reddish-blonde hair, the freckles across slightly-tipped nose. Pain started in Jim's throat, moved to his stomach and made him want to vomit.

Jim, himself, should be the Brogdon listed. He could almost read his own name there instead of Tommy's—James D. Brogdon, oldest son of Sam and Mary.

Mother had died understanding. On the farm when Dad had ordered Jim to kill a chicken for supper, Mother had always performed the chore for him. He simply couldn't kill! When Tommy had joined the army, Jim couldn't even bring himself to sign up as an ambulance driver. He froze at the sight of blood.

Dad would never, ever forgive him for fleeing to Canada to avoid the draft, for refusing to fight for a cause he couldn't bring himself to believe in. They had sat together at the Veteran's Hospital yesterday in stony silence or else they forced words like ping-pong balls back and forth across the card table of the quiet recreation room. Nurses had smiled at them—they looked as every father and son should look, like pals—but appearances weren't facts.

No Longer Drifting
Jackson-Britton

Jim's fingers returned to trace his brother's name on the stone monument. He should be dead and Tommy the one standing here!

Jim felt a coldness surge through him. What if Dad and all the rest were right? He should have sidestepped his heart-felt convictions and gone to war. It hadn't occurred to him then, but it did now. Now he lived in a state of constant self-condemnation.

"I knew him," said a voice from behind Jim. "Some kid! He never allowed us to get down. Tommy was always laughing."

Jim's hand shrank from Tommy's name. He forced himself to turn around and face a huge bulk of a man in a wheelchair. At first he didn't recognize him—his old buddy, Anthony Martin, who lived just around the section from the Brogdon farm. Then Jim felt a rush of joy, quickly blocked by the knowledge that Anthony's scorn for him would be much greater, and more meaningful than Dad's.

"Jim!" the big man cried. "It's been so long. I know you must be back in town." Anthony jerked the wheelchair forward with rapid thrusts from strong arms. Awkwardly Jim gripped the huge hand extended to him—coward to hero. Irony seemed as solid as the great stone monument bearing Tommy's name.

Jim looked deep into Anthony's eyes, as blue and fragile as a robin's eggs. In spite of his eyes, the creases in dark skin, deep furrows around narrow lips, suggested cynicism, a hardness Jim would never have believed possible in his boyhood chum.

"How is Rene?" Jim had been engaged to Anthony's sister, Rene, eight years ago when he had fled from Baxter County.

Coward. Coward. The word rang so loudly in Jim's mind that he could barely hear Anthony's answer. "She's fine. Got a little boy. Cody. Say, why don't you come out to the farm tonight and have dinner with us?"

Jim studied his old friend's face for some sign of judgment or scorn. Even though he saw none, he said, "Can't make it tonight."

"I think Rene would like to see you. You know, she and Mitchell split up a couple of years ago. She finally admitted she made a mistake."

Jim couldn't bring himself to answer. The town scalawag—how could Rene have married him in the first place? Jim's heart raged, just as it had the day the news of their marriage had reached him and now in the silence, he relived that moment.

"You can't be serious!" he had yelled at her on the phone.

He had not seen, but could visualize the way Rene must have raised her chin, hazel eyes snapping with anger. "At least he's going to Vietnam! And I'm marrying him before he leaves!"

No Longer Drifting
Jackson-Britton

"Don't do this to us, Rene! Live in Canada with me! I'll come get you!"

"You've ruined everything!" He had heard her sob, "You damned coward!" before she hung up.

Anthony's voice cut into the echoing memory of her words. "Mitchell's drinking gets worse and worse. When he gets drunk enough, he heads right out to the farm. Sometime, I swear, old Harriet and I are going to settle with him." He smiled a little. "Remember Harriet, my first rifle? Probably she's the only one that can persuade Mitchell to leave Windfield and let us alone."

"Do you think Rene would really want to see me?"

"Sure. Why not? Be there at six, Jim. It'll be like old times."

* * *

Jim's hand reached out to press the doorbell. His fingers felt stiff and cold, exactly as they had when he touched his brother's name on granite. He waited, listening as he used to do for Rene's lithe step, waiting expectantly for the warm smile on full red lips, the toss of long, straight hair. He loved her hair! Dark, but streaked with blonde, as if the sun itself had traced rays of light into its thick, heavy strands.

At last the door laboriously opened. Anthony awkwardly manipulated the wheelchair away to allow Jim to enter. It was the same cozy old farm-home, where as children they had sprawled before the huge fireplace with cards and checkers. Although no fire burned tonight, the room still smelled strongly of smoke. He looked around for Rene.

"She's went out," Anthony said glumly, then his tone changed to a forced exuberance. "Supper's ready to put on the table. After dinner I thought we'd play some chess. You still play chess, Jim?"

"I win more often playing poker," Jim said, trying to conceal the deep hurt Rene's absence caused him.

"Think twice before you take me on," Anthony advised. "I learned to play a mean game in Nam. And all that time in the hospital after the mine explosion while they pieced me back together again."

Jim did not tell Anthony that he had perfected his poker game in Canada, where days had stretched before him long and endless. He thought about his companions there, about shirkers and dope addicts, about the hippie zealots, none of whom made him feel comfortable. He usually ended up wondering if they were what they seemed to be…if he was.

Anthony transported the last dish to the table and looked at him. A glint of pity showed in the robin-egg-blue eyes. Jim didn't want Anthony's pity. He wanted him to understand. But he found he could confide in him no more than he could confide in his father or Rene.

Despite this, he started to speak about what he had done, but his words trailed off when a little boy of about four stormed into the room. He had big hazel eyes, like Rene's, and straight, dark hair. Jim's presence made him shy.

"This is Cody," Anthony said.

"Where's Mommy? Won't she eat with us?"

"Guess not, Cowboy. You washed up?"

Knowing Rene did not even want to see him stifled Jim's desire to eat. He forked the roast beef, sipped the strong coffee.

After dinner, Anthony said, "Come with me to get the cards. I want to show you my hobby."

Anthony wheeled to the threshold of the adjoining room where he waited for Jim to follow. "Wait till you see this, old buddy." Anthony opened the metal footlocker at the end of his bed. Looking over his shoulder, Jim saw row after row of silver bars.

"Aren't they beauts?" Anthony looked up at Jim, proud and eager for admiration. "Every spare minute of my time, I melt silver. For years I've been buying scraps of jewelry, anything silver. Fantastic, isn't it? What do you think?"

"I think that's a whole lot of value to be just lying around. You should get a safe."

Anthony laughed. "You've been away from Windfield way too long. This is the only place left in the States where you can leave your keys in the ignition and expect to drive away in the morning. Besides," he added, "if all else fails, I still have Harriet."

As he maneuvered through the small doorway back into the front room, Anthony gave a trustful glance at his old rifle, which hung low enough on the wall for him to reach.

Cody fell asleep on the couch, and Jim and Anthony played game after game of cards.

"What was it like? In Nam?" Jim ventured.

"It was hell. What was it like in Canada?"

"For me, the same. What's worse is that nothing gets any better." He tried to smile. "Coward, that's my permanent label. I might as well have it branded on my forehead."

Anthony chucked. "I wonder what should be stamped on mine? Despite my row of medals, I've played both roles. Don't even know which one's which anymore. I gunned down a host of enemies, but not because I'm a hero. It was an act of pure panic."

"But I wasn't even there…didn't even try…"

Anthony's eyes lifted from the cards; they appraised him in a mild, kindly way and he summed up his thoughts. "I was always too much the realist and you're too much the idealist. That's the real difference between us." He continued to study Jim. "I'm not saying you were right in what you did, but I know one thing, you thought you were right. And it takes real courage to go against what everyone else thinks."

Jim didn't deserve a friend like Anthony. Haunted more than ever by his long ago decision, he quickly looked away. Deep shame rose within him—Tommy was dead, his best friend was confined to a wheelchair. And he was stuck in a time zone far in the past, from which he would probably never break free.

* * *

Two days later Jim glimpsed Rene through the huge window of Cloy's I.G.A. She quickly pushed a cart down the aisle, decisively increasing her stock without ever really stopping. His heart hammered as he woodenly entered the store. She made a sharp turn down rows of canned goods, and he hurried to catch up. "Rene!"

The cart drew to an uncertain halt. Jim caught his breath at the shimmering of golden strands as she turned to him.

"I heard you were in town," she said hesitantly.

No warmth, no light, appeared in the hazel eyes.

"I've been visiting Dad. He's not doing too well."

"I know. I stop by to see him when I can."

"You look..." he wanted to say, 'as pretty as ever,' but his voice faltered, just as his hands did that started to reach out for her.

No Longer Drifting
Jackson-Britton

After an awkward silence, she said, "Jim, I have to go. I've got an appointment at ten." Without even a glance back, Rene guided the cart toward the checkout.

Jim lifted a magazine from the rack near him. She was just like Dad. She wasn't ever going to forgive or forget. Allowing her ample time to leave, he approached the window and watched her place the sacks into her car. Then he noticed her ex, Mitchell Gates.

Jim recognized him immediately, even though he was no longer the image of the lady's man. His hair and beard had become shaggy and unkempt. He was thinner, but the swagger was still present in his walk, more pronounced than ever. Jim watched him cut across the street toward Rene and felt himself stiffen. The look on Mitchell's face meant trouble.

Rene and he talked for a while, then Mitchell grabbed Rene's arms roughly as if they were arguing. It would soon get out of hand, Jim decided. Mitchell had progressed little from his old days as high school bully.

Jim emerged from the store, strode forward, and stood squarely before them. "Let go of her."

Daring anyone to interfere, Mitchell swung around to face him. When he did, a glint of sardonic recognition lit his eyes.

"Look who's here," he sing-songed. "When did you get back from the war?"

No Longer Drifting
Jackson-Britton

"I told you to let go of her."

"This is not your concern. This is between my wife and me."

"Not your wife any longer," Jim said quietly. Everything about Mitchell sickened Jim. The smell of staleness, of alcohol. "Is he bothering you, Rene?"

Before Rene could answer, Mitchell let her go and stepped forward. Scorn darkened Mitchell's eyes, enlarged the pupils, made them black. "If I was, what would you do about it?"

The word *you* sounded louder than the word *coward* ever had.

"Don't find out."

Mitchell advanced. "Go ahead. Hit me! That's what you want to do!"

Jim had never struck anyone in his life. He had never believed fighting and violence could resolve anything.

"What are you waiting for?" Mitchell taunted, gesturing for Jim to come closer. "What's wrong? You afraid of me?"

Anger blurred his eyes, caused a spinning to start in his head. He desperately wanted to grab Mitchell, to tear him limb for limb if that's what it took.

Mitchell waited. Rene did too, expectantly, scarcely breathing.

No Longer Drifting
Jackson-Britton

Why couldn't Jim move? Why did he just stand there staring at Mitchell, frozen?

"Why don't you two grow up," Rene snapped. With anger as evident as theirs, she climbed into the car and drove away.

* * *

Jim had to see Rene at least once before he left Windfield. He waited until he was certain she was home, then knocked at the door. In her pretty blue dress she looked as fresh and lovely as an afternoon in a summer garden.

She remained in the doorway. Anthony, behind her, called, "Jim! Come on in. You must have smelled the lasagna I'm cooking. In fact, you're just in time!"

"Don't tell me you can cook?"

Rene didn't want him here; that was perfectly plain. He was intruding for no good reason, just as he had intruded in front of the grocery store. Regardless, Jim stepped inside. "Where's Cody?"

"He has a slight fever. Rene put him to bed. Say, he'll like that," Anthony added, as he accepted the toy car Jim had brought for the boy and set it on the table.

"Cody looks exactly like you," Jim said to Rene.

She smiled a little. "I suppose that's possible."

During supper Jim thought that the ice in her manner was slowly beginning to thaw. She looked at him more often, even directed a question or two to him.

"Get out the old albums, Rene," Anthony said. "Jim and you can take a little trip down memory lane while I clear the table."

Obediently Rene found the albums and sitting a discreet distance from him on the couch began to turn pages. The scent of lilac perfume drifted to him.

They reviewed picture after picture—the ballgames, the senior prom, graduation. Could they ever have looked so young, been so happy?

Rene turned another page and Jim's eyes fell to a photograph of Tommy in uniform. It caused his throat to constrict. "Dad misses him so much," he said. "They always fished together and hunted."

"I know," Rene answered. "Your Dad seemed to die the same time Tommy did. His death must have been very hard on you, too. Everything must have been. Do you ever wish you had done…what everyone wanted you to do?"

Jim groped for an answer. What had once been clearly right or wrong, now seemed blurred. He started to speak, to tell her that, but was stopped by a fierce pounding on the front door.

Rene had snapped the chain lock after she had entered, so the partly open door jarred with each blow.

"It's Mitchell. Damn him! He must have followed you here." Anthony wheeled into the front room from the kitchen. "Don't answer it."

Jim's eyes left Anthony's hard face, riveted to the gun that hung on the wall close behind him.

They waited tensely. The pounding increased, each blow reverberating against wood and glass.

Mitchell's drunken voice cried, "Rene! We're going to have it out, once and for all! Open the door!"

Jim got to his feet. So did Rene. She shrank away, then stopped just in front of the room where Cody was sleeping.

For a few minutes there was silence, then a battering at the door. The chain lock broke loose, dangled downward, spilling screws to the floor.

Mitchell was drunk, but about him was a manner beyond drunkenness—an irrational state, almost insanity. "I'm leaving town," he said. "You and Cody are coming with me!"

"You know better than that," Rene replied, her voice high-pitched with fear.

"You heard her. Now just get out of here," Anthony said.

"I'm not leaving without you, Rene," he threatened, stepping deeper into the room. "Now, get the kid, or go without him."

No Longer Drifting
Jackson-Britton

"I'm not going anywhere. And you won't get far, either. Not without money."

Mitchell struck the table with his fist. The toy car Jim and brought for Cody rolled forward and fell to the floor.

"Then we'll just take those silver bars with us. That ought to start us up somewhere."

Anthony's voice sounded deadly. "You're not taking anything from this house!"

"Who's going to stop me?" He glanced scornfully from one man to the other. "A cripple? A coward?"

Anthony gave a quick twist to the wheel of his chair. It spun around and at the same time he reached for the rifle.

Mitchell lunged forward, hastening to capitalize on his great advantage. Much stronger, he wrested the gun from Anthony's hands. He aimed it at Anthony. Rene let out a startled scream.

At the same instant, Jim dived toward Mitchell. He tore the rifle from his hands and kicked it aside. Rene quickly retrieved it. The two of them faced-off, Jim calm, Mitchell enraged.

Jim was so used to condemning himself. But at that moment, he knew he wasn't now and never had been a coward. Fear for himself—that had never had anything to do with his decision not to fight in the war.

No Longer Drifting
Jackson-Britton

He grabbed Mitchell's shoulders, whirled him around, and sent him sprawling backward. Mitchell hit his head against the wooden arm of the couch. Dazed, he attempted to rise, but before he could stagger to his feet, Jim dragged him out the door and sent him hurling into the darkness toward his car.

"Get out of here while you can," Jim ordered.

Mitchell got to his feet and staggered toward his car. He didn't stop or look back, just got inside and drove away.

Jim watched the vehicle disappear from view. He hadn't changed his mind about anything; he still abhorred violence. But he understood now what he hadn't understood when he had evaded the draft— sometimes a man must fight back, sometimes he has no other choice.

A difficult concept, Jim thought, for a faithful pacifist. What Anthony had told him wasn't far wrong, he concluded, as he went back to the house. He had done what he had thought right at the time he had fled to Canada, and he had done the same thing tonight.

Rene rushed forward. "You saved us, Jim," she cried. "No telling what Mitchell would have done if you hadn't gotten that gun away from him."

"He's not likely to come out here again," Jim said.

"I think you're right," Anthony agreed. "Mitchell is gone for good." His robin-egg-blue eyes shifted from Rene to Jim as he added, "And I think, my friend, that you're back for good."

No Longer Drifting
Jackson-Britton

Two of Kelsey's inner personalities are vying for control of her. But which will prevail--the Cheerleader, or the Angel of Darkness?

ANGEL OF DARKNESS

The thought came to her when she was walking across the bridge on the way to the party. It had crept into her mind unaware, a free-floating thought, drifting loose and isolated as the patches of ice upon the gray-white river. A moment of wondering what it would be like just to drift away, to let the current carry her out to the deepest part—past the point of no return.

What good was life without Mark? What was the point of going to still another party, one she dreaded? What was the point, really, of going on?

Kelsey knew it was the Angel of Darkness who had

put these thoughts into her mind. Lately, the Angel had gradually been taking control. She could almost see her dark form merged with the mist from the river, beckoning.

Kelsey turned away, her footsteps quickening. By the time she reached the haven of light, the dark angel was gone.

***

"Kelsey's here!" she called from the doorway.

Her Cheerleader self was back, and Kelsey's relief at her well-timed arrival was mingled with a vague sense of foreboding. Kelsey could sense the Cheerleader taking charge, slowly gaining power over her. She felt the bubbling laughter rise up in her throat, heard the voice that wasn't quite her own respond to bright holiday greetings.

"Glad you could make it!" her boss, Ned Buchannan met her at the door. "I've got a big surprise for you!" Ned confided as he took her coat and led her further into the crowded room.

"You know how I love surprises!"

Her boss looked a little like Santa Claus, Kelsey couldn't help thinking. A few drinks always made his round face florid and merry.

"Someone here is just dying to meet you. One of my new executives." Ned's eyes sparkled mischievously. "I know you two will hit it off great.

No Longer Drifting
Jackson-Britton

"I hope he's not as bad as the last guy you set me up with," Kelsey wrinkled her nose. "I could have done better on a blind date." Because she lived just over the bridge from him, the boss had grown to count on her to welcome and entertain the occasional odd-man-out at his house parties. Often, like tonight, Kelsey didn't want to go. At other times she found it preferable to being alone and brooding about Mark.

"My own wife calls this one a hunk," Ned whispered under his breath. Kelsey spotted a pair of dark eyes glancing anxiously their way, was pleased when Ned waved an attractive young man over.

"Jeff Martin, this is Kelsey Burke." Introduction made, Ned slipped off toward the guestroom where the wraps were stored, Kelsey's coat slung casually over his arm. His absence virtually thrust her into the company of the tall, brown-haired man in a deep navy pullover and khaki chinos.

Kelsey was not surprised to feel an instant spark of attraction as the warm, dark eyes met hers. It seemed her fate to be drawn to rugged, well-muscled men, men who subtly reminded her of Mark.

"Ned's been telling me all about you," Jeff said.

"Oh, really? What did he say?" She could feel her throat tighten. She feared Ned might have told him too much. Kelsey, the recent divorcee, the *cheerleader*, who loved to dance and who couldn't hold her liquor.

No Longer Drifting
Jackson-Britton

After the divorce, Kelsey at times allowed the cheerleader to make her decisions for her. The faces of the men she met at bars and parties after work blurred together in her mind, none distinct, only temporary cures for night after night of unbearable loneliness. She no longer believed in love. But since Mark had left her, the need for arms to hold her in the night sometimes became unbearable.

Jeff smiled, his brown eyes lighting with mirth. "No need to look so serious. He said that you had green eyes, you're twenty-seven, and single. I'm new in town. That was enough to spark my interest. Unless—"he added with a touch of drama. "Unless you're hiding some deep, dark secret."

"No secrets." She returned his smile, then looked away. She could hardly tell him about her private demons, the ones she called the Cheerleader and the Angel of Darkness. Since the divorce, they had been appearing more and more frequently until they had become almost constant companions.

"We're about the only two singles here," Kelsey said. "And Ned's pretty obviously thrown us together."

"I don't mind." Jeff's eyes left her face, admiring the sexy red dress, and returned slightly more intimate. "Unless you do."

Kelsey's green eyes were encouraging. "Why don't you get us some drinks, then? I'll wait for you here."

No Longer Drifting
Jackson-Britton

"Okay." Kelsey watched Jeff's broad shoulders as he disappeared into the adjoining room where Ned's well-stocked bar was located. She saw anxiousness in his eyes as he glanced back at her, as if he were afraid that she might have slipped away. She forced a smile and tossed him a little wave. Tonight, she would be what everyone wanted her to be: bubbly, effervescent Kelsey—the Cheerleader. The smile faded as he moved out of sight. It was getting harder and harder to keep up the charade.

Kelsey stepped over to look out of the big picture window. Although it was warm inside, a layer of frost brushed the glass. Beyond were patches of snow and the bare gray branches of the trees that lined the river.

Within the house, Christmas tree lights blinked, showering her with rainbow colors. The sight of bright packages intensified the aching from within. She had bought an old-fashioned picture once at an auction—a man and woman sitting comfortably by the fireplace, two children playing at their feet. Home, family, security—she had wanted all that with Mark.

But then she had found out that she could never have children. And he had left her. She had tried to discuss with him the possibility of adoption, but to no avail. She remembered his last words to her, "Maybe I'm selfish, but I want kids of my own, not some stranger's baby."

Thoughts of Mark filled her with the usual thoughts of worthlessness and rejection. She had grown up with Mark, went to grade school with him, they had married right out of high school. His abandonment had left her without goals and identity.

Once more, Kelsey's eyes turned toward the river as if she would find an answer in the restless gray water. Hovering above its banks, the Angel of Darkness still seemed to beckon.

"Kelsey?" Jeff returned with two glasses of champagne. Startled, she turned toward him, just in time to see the beginnings of a frown crease his forehead. "Is something wrong, Kelsey?"

"Why, no. Of course not." She parted her lips to force another smile. The Cheerleader again, driving her on, covering her unhappiness with a false show of bravado. Sometimes friend rather than enemy. Sometimes, it was the Cheerleader who saved her. She took one of the crystal glasses from him. "Why would you think anything was wrong?"

He shrugged. "I don't know. Just the way you were standing there all alone, so sad, staring out of the window."

"I was watching the river." Kelsey took a sip of the bubbly champagne. The taste of it fortified her, made her feel bolder. "On the way to the party, I stopped and looked down from the bridge."

No Longer Drifting
Jackson-Britton

Jeff was watching her with dark, serious eyes.

Even though she could hear the sounds of voices and laughter all around them, it seemed as if the two of them were all alone. She had a sudden impulse to tell him how she had felt, to let him know of her thoughts while staring down, hypnotized, from the bridge. But, of course, he wouldn't understand. "The view was lovely," she finished quickly.

"You walked here, then," Jeff said. "So did I."

"I live in the Westhill apartments."

"Then that makes us almost neighbors." He gave a little frown. "I'll walk you home later. That bridge is so slick and icy it could be dangerous."

"Don't worry about me," Kelsey said with a lift of her chin. "I'm used to the cold. I grew up in Minnesota."

"I came from California," Jeff replied. "This cold weather is still a new experience for me."

In an attempt at small talk, she asked, "So, what brings you here to New York, Jeff?"

For a moment, he seemed reluctant to reply. "I was in a relationship." He seemed not to want to talk about it, as if it were too painful. "It didn't work out. I needed a change of scene." He turned her question. "But I'd rather talk about you. I want to know all about you!"

"Nothing much to tell," Kelsey replied, feeling

herself slipping into gloom again.

Sporadic bursts of music interrupted their conversation. Someone in the next room, trying to decide which songs to play. Good! There would be dancing soon. Drink and dancing. No more talk.

Kelsey finished her champagne and set the glass down next to Jeff's empty one on the coffee table. The chatter of voices all around them was gone. Music from the large, adjoining room played loud and steady now, with no interruptions. Kelsey glanced up, surprised to find that most of the crowd had drifted toward the music. She and Jeff were nearly alone.

"Shall we dance?"

"Sure." Jeff sounded slightly disappointed, as if he might have preferred to linger and talk a little more. She took his arm, drawing him with her toward the music.

She was glad for the crowded room, the endless music, the lights that flickered and blinked. The huge hall—Ned's pride and joy—was set up like a private disco, complete with neon lights and stereo, tables, and private bar. Often these past few months, places like this, where she felt free to be someone other than herself, had been Kelsey's haven.

Soothed by the wine, she closed her eyes and leaned her head on Jeff's shoulder. She felt his hands, light and lingering, upon the small of her back. Kelsey marveled at how easy it would be to love a stranger. As long as she kept things impersonal, there were no ugly emotions to deal with, no hurt and anger like there had been with Mark. She sighed, wishing the dance would go on forever.

The music kept changing. Kelsey felt a moment of uneasiness when a man wearing a cowboy hat tried to cut in. She stiffened in Jeff's arms as she recognized Derek, one of the men she had met in a local bar. He had been drunk and obnoxious the miserable evening they had spent together. And he didn't look too sober tonight.

"Be a sport," she heard him urge, nudging Jeff. She hated the way he grinned, the uneven way his lips exposed chipped, cigarette-stained teeth. "Share the wealth. Let me dance a round or two with Kelsey here."

"Sorry, Pal. She's with me."

"Don't kid yourself. Kelsey belongs to everyone!"

Kelsey felt her face burn as Jeff pretended not to hear. He held her even tighter as they moved away. She saw Derek glaring after them, his ferret-like eyes darting and angry. But finally, he moved on.

After several more dances, they settled into one of the tables in the corner. "I'll get us some more drinks," Jeff said.

Kelsey sat waiting, listening to the music. Jeff was

gone a long time. She glanced anxiously toward the bar, where she spotted him in the far corner, talking to a young blonde woman in a black silk dress. The girl had her hand on his arm; their heads were close together. The sight brought back painful memories of her seeing Mark passing his phone number to other women, making dates behind her back. Mark's many betrayals had sown the ugly seeds of suspicion. Surely, Jeff was slipping this girl his number now.

Jeff came back with the drinks and sat down beside her. An awkward silence followed. A silence that Jeff, no doubt, had expected would be filled with light-hearted banter and entertaining company. The confrontation with Derek and the sight of Jeff's flirting with the blonde woman had left Kelsey moody and silent.

Kelsey took the last sip of her drink, trying to prolong the glow, but the Cheerleader was rapidly deserting her. She was aware of her self-induced sense of well being eroding away, leaving a dull, aching throb like the beginnings of a headache. This was what she hated most about the Cheerleader. She always abandoned her without warning, leaving her at the mercy of the Angel of Darkness.

She could see Jeff watching her with a deep, concerned expression. "I want to get to know you, Kelsey," he said. "Why won' t you talk to me? I have a feeling I'm not seeing the real you."

"This is the real me." The hardness in her voice seemed to surprise Jeff.

She detected a puzzled, almost hurt look in his eyes. She looked away from him, but sensed that he was still watching her, watching in that curious, alarmed way that everyone watched the decline of the Cheerleader. It was a werewolf-like transformation. She couldn't let him witness it.

"I've got to go to the ladies' room," she murmured, pulling back her chair. Her voice sounded choked and strange. A slight dizziness buzzed in her brain—maybe the result of too many drinks. "I'll be right back."

As she walked away from him, she knew that she would not return. Her chest had tightened until it was difficult to draw a breath. She could not stay at the party and let Jeff see her mask slip. The ghastly depression she had been warding off all evening had arrived with the force of a blustering snowstorm. Not even the Cheerleader could save her now.

She did not meet anyone as she made her escape from the side door of the house. The air outside was nippy, biting. Her bare shoulders were chilled. She had forgotten her coat, but she wouldn't go back for it now. Like one in a trance, she hurried across the crusted mounds of cold earth, feeling the occasional shock of snow against the back of her high heels.

Kelsey reached the bridge. She stood silently for a moment. Turning, she could still see the lights of the party, but as if from far away. She paused to glance downward where chunks of ice flowed sluggishly past, carried downstream by the flowing current. Only a jagged slope of earth separated her from the swirling gray water.

What did she have to live for? She stared down, weaving a little, like someone transfixed. She had always been terrified of guns, wary of pills, but water inspired in her no fear, no particular revulsion. Just a sinking. A soft, silky sinking into a watery grave where the Angel of Darkness waited.

Kelsey had to get away from here! Her heel caught as she started across the bridge. In her haste to free herself, she lost her footing. The sudden jolt took her by surprise. Suddenly, she felt herself sliding on the glass-slick surface, down the slope of impacted snow beneath the high, metal guardrail. Emitting a startled cry, she reached out for the railing, but could not keep hold of it. As if in a dream, she found herself slipping down through layers of darkness and mist into the freezing water.

Die? Isn't that what you wanted? Isn't that what you've wished for all along?

The shock of cold water revived her. In spite of the

No Longer Drifting
Jackson-Britton

echoing words of the Angel of Darkness, Kelsey, choking and gasping, fought her way to the surface.

Her senses sprang vividly to life. The instinct to survive became a driving force.

The current had pulled her away from the shoreline. Now, she caught a glimpse of the cloudy bank that suddenly seemed miles away from her. She wasn't much of a swimmer. Could she make it back?

A sudden surge of panic held her motionless. She wasn't going to reach safety. She was going to sink again into that watery grave!

In that icy neverland, both the Angel of Darkness and the Cheerleader had deserted her. There was only Kelsey Burke, and she wanted so desperately to live!

Her will grew stronger, drowning the haunting darkness and mist. Hands and legs flayed, expending useless energy. Still, she kept on struggling to keep her head above water, forcing her arms and legs to keep moving until her lungs threatened to burst.

A stab of panic filled her as she realized she could no longer see the shoreline. She had lost all sense of direction. Was she going toward the bank or swimming away from it? Once again her frantic thrashing motions ceased. Useless to even try. She felt herself getting weaker. Better to drift along with the current. She sank, managed to rise again.

"Kelsey!"

No Longer Drifting
Jackson-Britton

Had she imagined the sound of her name being called? Far away she could see the hazy edges of the shore, a form cloaked in fog, barely visible on the bank.

Struggling to stay afloat, she turned her ear instinctively toward the sound.

Again, she heard her name. "Kel—sey!

With renewed hope and effort, she began once more to swim. She was going to save herself. She was going to live!

A splash cut through the silence. She was aware that someone was plunging in, attempting to meet her midway.

She felt strong, supporting arms reaching out for her. Easily now, they propelled themselves to the bank. Breathless, shivering, she collapsed against him.

Jeff didn't speak. He guided her up the steep embankment toward the top of the bridge. She had the sensation of breaking through the grips of the past, of rising above the mist, just as she was, in reality, doing now.

Jeff hurried to wrap something warm around her. "When I saw that you'd left, I came after you," he said. "I remembered how icy the bridge was and I saw that you'd left your coat."

Moonlight glowed across his face, across the damp, dark hair that fell across his forehead. His voice seemed to break. "I saw you up there on the bridge, saw you fall."

His understanding eyes held hers. They were nice eyes, filled with tenderness and compassion. The eyes did not remind her of Mark at all.

She tried to speak, to find the words to thank him, but her lips were chattering too much from the cold. Suddenly, he pulled her into his arms. Both half-frozen, they clung together.

"I've got to get you somewhere warm and dry," he whispered. But he held her tightly, as if he never intended to let her go.

As they moved away, Kelsey only glanced back once to look at the river. The mist had cleared forever. She was stronger than she ever dreamed she could be. And free, free to live her life successfully as Kelsey Burke, alone, if need be.

In her heart, she knew that some driving force from deep inside herself had kept her from drowning tonight. The Cheerleader? Kelsey smiled a little. No, it had been the real Kelsey Burke who had saved herself tonight. Somehow, from this moment on, she knew she would not be hearing from either the Angel of Darkness or the Cheerleader again. She didn't need them anymore.

No Longer Drifting
Jackson-Britton

John deeply regretted the estrangement from his brother, Matt, the years of constant quarreling, fed by murky, unspoken undercurrents.

A NEW YEAR

Forgive and forget—John had wanted to do just that. After all, Matt was his brother, the only close relative he had left. Among friends and acquaintances only a few remained who really remembered Mom and Dad, the farm, the days of skipping school, swimming in the river. Or his tedious climb up the ladder to reach a success John now found so frighteningly empty.

"Christmas dinner at the farm," Matt had said on the phone,

"like the old days…"

No Longer Drifting
Jackson-Britton

John had despised the hesitation in his own voice as he had answered. "One o'clock all right?"

Matt would know John would be early. Being early, and ahead of others in thought and action, accounted for his position as president of Brenton Investment. It allowed him to rent the luxurious condominium overlooking the Missouri River, to drive the Cadillac that strained now, swaying to follow the ruts that tires had cut deep into mud and gravel.

During the long ride from Kansas City, which had given him ample time to think, the desire for forgiveness and its actual accomplishment had separated into two issues. As John drew closer to the farm, the terrible words, the clash of wills that had flared at Mother's death and that had blazed repeatedly in the years following, paraded before him like some triumphant army, too massive, too powerful for any counter-attack to be likely or even possible.

John glimpsed his own image in the rear-view mirror as he reached to switch off the key. Except for the rimless glasses, the touch of gray at his temples, he appeared quite the same. Perhaps a little more stern, a little less inclined to smile.

But in the old days he would have been able to smell the aroma of mince pies, the spicy odor of cooking turkey. The mere sight of the slightly sagging, two-story house would have impelled him forward.

No Longer Drifting
Jackson-Britton

Today he felt halting, indecisive, abandoned by the confident assurance he so easily claimed.

Matt came out of the back door, shirt sleeves rolled up, shivering against the sharp north wind that left flakes of snow visible on his thick, dark hair.

Somberly staring at the ground beginning to whiten, Matt made the hesitant suggestion, "Let's not talk business."

What else did John have to discuss? His wife, many years dead, no children—all life was joyless and vacant beyond the plush office where he ruled alone.

The brothers had fought. First over the farm that Mom had left solely to Matt, her youngest, then over the firm Dad had started—where the two of them could compete openly and where John, quicker to see and turn an advantage, had taken over.

Still, the farm had been John's first love. He had always run it, but Dad had died first. How could Mom have spread John's lowly place in her affections so blatantly before the world? Yes, she had given the excuse of Matt's wife, Jill, of his three sons and their need for security, but the wound still bled whenever he returned.

As they entered the house, a memory of Mom's face, shiny from the hot kitchen, topped with soft, gray curls, rose to his mind and brought with it increased pain. For a moment John felt the threat of his emotions being revealed. Then the face slowly became Jill's.

"Hello, John," Matt's wife said warmly. "So glad you could come."

It had been many years since he had eaten dinner at the farm. He managed an answering smile, discerning that Jill regretted the years of constant quarreling, fed by murky, unspoken undercurrents.

A crowd of kitchen workers was busy cutting pies and chopping great mounds of vegetables. Why, he could hardly remember which woman had married which of Matt and Jill's sons.

Suddenly, it seemed important to him. He stopped beside the young woman in jeans and baggy shirt, all legs and arms. "You're... Allison."

She giggled. "No, Barb. Allison's over there." She directed the knife she held toward the stove where another young woman, a little taller and much thinner, was taking a roaster from the oven.

"Well, Merry Christmas," John said, then added to himself, *whoever you are.*

Matt, a little edgy, waited for him to enter the front room. John wandered toward the Christmas tree, shapeless and shaggy, cut from the pasture. He should have thought to bring gifts.

John could feel Matt watching him. In the stillness he longed to return to where they had been a long time ago. He remembered the family attending church together—the candle-lit altar, the harmony of voices, the rising above what was frail and human.

But he might as well be realistic. The gulf between Matt and him had existed too long and was now too wide to bridge. John's gray eyes rose to the star that twinkled at the top of the tree. Perhaps no forgiveness was possible without divine intervention.

"You want to listen to the game?" Matt asked.

"I don't. Usually. Whatever you want." The indecisiveness had surfaced again and sounded in his voice.

Matt made no attempt to reach for the remote control. The room sank deep into layers of uneasy silence.

John didn't belong here any longer. The formality of the dinner table convinced him of that. Matt's sons had changed, taken on Matt's width and ruggedness. Time passed so quickly. How could he have missed their growing up—the camping trips, the sport's activities? They could have been like his own sons, not strangers who directed to him polite questions in an attempt to breech the great distance.

John's thoughts drifted to his office. He would stop there on the way home and pick up some work for the evening. He would welcome the stacks of contracts. With them, he could respond safely, confidently.

No Longer Drifting
Jackson-Britton

When the long dinner ended, Matt, acting sad and disheartened, ushered him back into the front room. Their reunion wasn't going well, wasn't what either of them had wanted.

John passed the Christmas tree, not glancing toward it, but aware of the star that sent beams of yellow light spasmodically across the room. For a long time he stood by the window, looking past the huge, drooping barn toward the fields where he had invested so much of his youth. The home place—it still meant so much to him! He hated the fact that Matt was not keeping it up.

"It looks as if you're going to have to repair the barn," he said.

John started to go on, but Matt stopped him, a tinge of harshness in his voice. "I don't want to worry about the farm today."

John fell silent, resenting the rebuff, thinking about how much Matt owed him. A Christmas dinner wouldn't begin to pay him back. Not a lifetime of Christmas dinners! The farm would have failed time and again without the checks John himself had written, checks that had bought him... what?

"I'd probably better be going," John said, trying to keep his voice from sounding cold. "I have work to do."

"On Christmas?" Matt eased himself into the recliner and absently lifted one of his grandchildren to his knee. "Jill will be disappointed. She spent a lot of time digging pictures and keepsakes out of Mom's trunk to show you."

John's gaze fell to a cardboard box on the coffee table overflowing with old photographs and letters. He forced himself to sit stiffly on the couch within their easy reach.

He had seen them a thousand times, still, he opened a worn album and glanced at a picture of himself as a gangly boy, trying to teach Matt to swim. Matt had always been so eager to follow his lead. It seemed several lifetimes ago—the days when Matt had trusted him.

John shuffled through numerous pages, pausing to say with a half-smile, "Remember our boat?"

"How could I forget it! Whenever I get to thinking I'm smart, that boat returns as a reminder. How many times did it sink, anyway?"

"*Every* time," John answered. "We should have forgotten the old structure and started all over."

Matt's voice sounded very grave. "You were never willing to do that," he said.

Did Matt blame him for all the good years the two of them had lost? To refocus his thoughts, John hurriedly opened an envelope—a letter Mother had started to her sister, years ago, during her last illness. He skimmed it, eyes returning to reread lines written

No Longer Drifting
Jackson-Britton

about him. "John is so strong. I never have any doubts about John. He will be sure to carry on. I can depend on John to take care of everything Ted and I love."

Thoughtfully John folded the letter and placed it back in the envelope.

He looked up, watching Matt. The grandchild—was this one Donna?—snuggled, safe, half-asleep, in the circle of his arms.

Mother would have no complaints. He had saved the farm and had turned the company into one of national reputation. Still, for an instant, doubts began to assail him.

From the depths of his own misgivings came a clear realization: he had spent years and years taking care of all the wrong things. What Mom and Dad had loved had been neither the farm nor Brenton Investment.

John met Matt's dark eyes and read in them his own question: where did they go from here? John pondered this for a moment, then his gaze shifted from his brother to the star at the top of the crudely decorated Christmas tree. As he watched the light blink on and off, he suddenly understood.

The End

ABOUT THE AUTHORS

Loretta Jackson and Vickie Britton are a sister co-authoring team whose over thirty published novels include mysteries and romantic suspense. Two of their mystery-romance novels Path of the Jaguar and Nightmare in Morocco have gone into second printings. Their works have been produced in paper, audio and electronic format. They enjoy writing short stories and have two new titles coming out this year from Whiskey Creek Press, a mainstream anthology NO LONGER DRIFTING, and a collection of suspense stories THE BLOODY KNIFE.

Vickie Britton

Vickie Britton lives in the beautiful mountain town of Laramie, Wyoming, with her husband, Roger, where they own and operate a local computer store. Their son, Ed, is a student at the Colorado Institute of Art in Denver, where he is studying graphic art and animation. Vickie has a degree in British Literature and has taken many courses in criminal justice, forensics, and police science.

Loretta Jackson

Loretta Jackson lives in Junction City, Kansas where she manages real estate and writes full-time. A former teacher, she taught high school English and Creative Writing on the Pine Ridge Indian Reservation in Wanblee, South Dakota. Loretta and her sister and co-author Vickie Britton travel to exotic locations, lately to Russia, China and Peru, to research settings for their novels. Most of their books are adventure and suspense-- the Ardis Cole Mystery Series, and PATH OF THE JAGUAR. Their most recent work, NO LONGER DRIFTING and THE BLOODY KNIFE, both from Whiskey Creek, are collections of short stories.

For your reading pleasure, we welcome you to visit our web bookstore

WHISKEY CREEK PRESS

www.whiskeycreekpress.com